SPECIAL MESSAGE TO READERS

THE ULVERSCROFT FOUNDATION
(registered UK charity number 264873)
was established in 1972 to provide funds for research, diagnosis and treatment of eye diseases. Examples of major projects funded by the Ulverscroft Foundation are:-

- The Children's Eye Unit at Moorfields Eye Hospital, London
- The Ulverscroft Children's Eye Unit at Great Ormond Street Hospital for Sick Children
- Funding research into eye diseases and treatment at the Department of Ophthalmology, University of Leicester
- The Ulverscroft Vision Research Group, Institute of Child Health
- Twin operating theatres at the Western Ophthalmic Hospital, London
- The Chair of Ophthalmology at the Royal Australian College of Ophthalmologists

You can help further the work of the Foundation by making a donation or leaving a legacy. Every contribution is gratefully received. If you would like to help support the Foundation or require further information, please contact:

THE ULVERSCROFT FOUNDATION
The Green, Bradgate Road, Anstey
Leicester LE7 7FU, England
Tel: (0116) 236 4325

website: www.foundation.ulverscroft.com

I'M WATCHING YOU

Lauren Bradley lives a quiet life in her village flat, with only her cat for company. So why would anyone choose her as a target for stalking? As the harassment becomes increasingly disturbing, several possible candidates emerge. Could it be Lauren's old friend, Greg, who now wants more than just friendship? Sam, the shy man who works in the butcher's shop across the street and seems to know her daily routine? Or even handsome but ruthless Nicholas Jordan, her new boss to whom she is dangerously, but hopelessly, attracted?

Books by Susan Udy
in the Linford Romance Library:

THE CALL OF THE PEACOCK
FORTUNE'S BRIDE
DARK FORTUNE
DANGEROUS LEGACY
REBELLIOUS HEARTS
SUSPICIOUS HEART
TENDER TAKEOVER
DARK SUSPICION
CLIFF HOUSE
THE UNFORGIVING HEART
THE RELUCTANT STAND-IN

SUSAN UDY

I'M WATCHING YOU

Complete and Unabridged

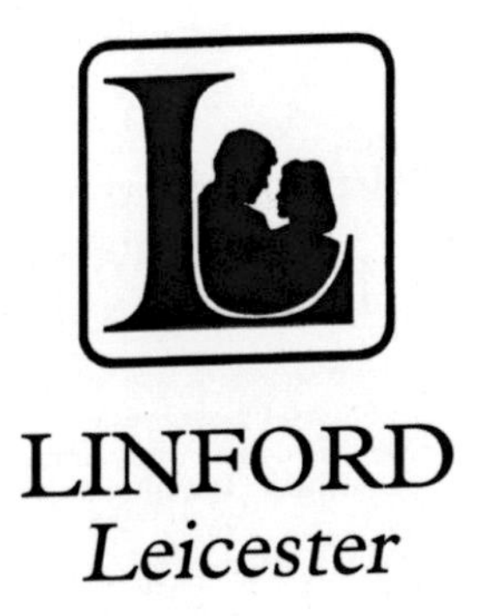

LINFORD
Leicester

First published in Great Britain in 2015

First Linford Edition
published 2015

A catalogue record for this book is available from the British Library.

ISBN 978–1–4448–2409–4

Published by
F. A. Thorpe (Publishing)
Anstey, Leicestershire

Set by Words & Graphics Ltd.
Anstey, Leicestershire
Printed and bound in Great Britain by
T. J. International Ltd., Padstow, Cornwall

This book is printed on acid-free paper

1

Eleven o'clock in the evening.

He sat, completely motionless, cocooned within the confines of the car, staring upwards at the curtained window on the other side of the street.

Where was she?

He knew she was in there; he could see the glow of a light. All of a sudden the curtain was pulled to one side and there she was, standing, looking down on him.

Good, she knew he was here, watching her; that he'd always be watching her.

That was enough for now.

* * *

Lauren Bradley dragged the curtain of her first floor window to one side and peered out. She gasped and instinctively pulled backwards before telling herself not to be so stupid; she had a perfect right to look out of her own window. She leant forward once more.

It was there again and although she couldn't see it clearly, she was sure it was the same car.

In which case, that made it the fourth — or was it the fifth? — night in a row that it had parked in the same position, at the same time. The first evening it had happened she'd been on the point of going to bed when she'd been distracted by the sound of a car engine noisily revving in the street beneath her flat. She'd gone to the window, wondering who could be making such a racket at this time of night.

Over the couple of years that she'd been living here she'd grown to recognise the cars that regularly parked down there overnight, and this particular vehicle wasn't one of them.

That had been unusual enough, but what really grabbed her attention was the sight of the driver sitting inside, not making any move to get out; not making any move at all. In fact, he stayed unnaturally still. In the end she'd assumed he was waiting for someone, and when she'd checked again half an hour later and saw that the car had gone, she presumed her assumption had been the right one.

She'd thought no more about it until the following evening. Again, she'd been about to go to bed when she'd heard the same revving. She'd looked out and there it had been, the identical car — at eleven o'clock exactly. And it had happened every night since.

She frowned now. Who on earth could it be? And why was he there again? If he was waiting for someone, he wasn't having much luck. She knew that because on the previous evening she'd stood in the window, careful to remain behind the partially drawn curtain, and simply watched. No one had joined him; he'd remained completely alone.

It was at that point that she began to question the reason for its presence on the street. And question the fact that each time, the driver had parked opposite her flat, positioned — deliberately? she wondered now — in between the street lights with its own lights extinguished, thus making it impossible for Lauren to see who was in the driving seat. All she'd been able to make out was a dark shape, a man's shape she thought, but she supposed it could be a large woman. Also, no matter how she strained her eyes, she couldn't distinguish the number plate, the colour — it could be blue, grey, anything — or even the make of car. Not that she was any sort of expert on cars. They were all much of a muchness nowadays. It was small, she could see that, but it could be any one of the hatchbacks that were to be seen everywhere.

Whatever or whoever it was, the suspicion began to take root that it was her flat the driver was concentrating on.

There was something about the way he was sitting, leaning forward slightly, head tilted, as if his gaze were fixed on her window. What she didn't know was why whoever it was should be out there, motionless and watching.

Could it be the police, carrying out some sort of undercover surveillance operation in an unmarked car? Could she be under suspicion for some sort of crime? Well if she was, they'd got the wrong woman. She'd never broken the law, not in all of her twenty-nine years. Maybe they were watching one of her neighbours?

She snorted. That was equally ridiculous. She'd put money on all of her neighbours also being honest, law-abiding people.

Maybe she should go out and confront the driver? Demand to know what he or she was doing there each evening at this particular time? But supposing it was some sort of weird Peeping Tom? Maybe she should ring the police instead. They were always asking people to notify them of any sort of suspicious behaviour, and this was definitely suspicious.

She glanced up and down the street, or as much of it as she could see from her limited vantage point, but it was deserted — which, let's face it, it usually was at this time of night.

Lower Markham wasn't the hottest of nightspots. Far from it. It was a sleepy village populated by people who only wanted a quiet life, most of them considerably older than Lauren. Its single main street was lined solely with shops rather than cafes and bars, all with flats above them, and the only pub was the old-fashioned, traditional sort at the far end, all oak beams and stained walls; although it was rather daringly named the Frog and Spawn, local people usually referred to it as the Frog.

All of which meant that there'd most likely be no one to help her if she went out and managed to land herself in some sort of trouble.

But even as she had the thought, the vehicle's headlights blazed and the car began to move. The lights flashed twice, as if the driver were bidding her farewell, before it accelerated along the road beneath her to disappear around the bend that led out of the village. And once again, no one had joined the driver; she was positive about that. So why had he been there, other than to watch her flat?

She closed the curtains and walked back into the room, snorting at her own foolishness. She'd always had a vivid imagination, but this — well, this was bordering on fantasy. Why would someone be watching her, police or otherwise? Yet, the driver had flashed his lights — at her? Or someone else? Could it have been a neighbour under surveillance, after all? Or had it been some sort of signal?

If it was, it couldn't have been to one of the shops. They were all closed at this time of night, their lights switched off, everyone long since gone, even the

Indian grocer. Anyway, the police wouldn't broadcast their presence by the flashing of their lights; they'd just leave. No, the more she considered events, the more convinced she became that it hadn't been an unmarked police car.

She returned to the settee and the television. If she was being watched, or maybe even stalked — after all, you did hear of such things nowadays — who on earth could it be? And why? Could it be someone she'd upset or offended at some time? Unlikely. She certainly couldn't recall anything of that nature.

'What do you think, Sheba?'

She looked down at the beautiful blue-grey cat curled at her side and began to fondle the animal's silky smooth fur. Eighteen months ago, feeling the need for some sort of company to alleviate her solitary state, she'd decided she needed a pet and she'd gone along to a local cat rescue centre and chosen Sheba from twenty-five or so other animals. She'd been cruelly treated by the teenage son of a local family — Lauren didn't know who — and in the end they'd turned her out to fend for herself. She'd eventually been picked up, half-starved, with dull, patchy fur, and taken to the rescue centre where the owner had nursed her back to health. For Lauren — and, she suspected, Sheba too — it had been love at first sight.

Sheba now meowed at her as if to say, 'Well, don't ask me. I don't know,' and jumped off the settee. She then raised her tail perpendicularly — something she always did when irritated — twitched it back and forth, as if to endorse her cry of annoyance, and finally stalked off towards the kitchen where she knew she'd find her bowl of food.

Lauren smiled fondly. At times her pet appeared to be almost human, letting her mistress know unequivocally when she was displeased with her — usually when her food didn't appear quickly enough — but that aside, she was great company. In fact, Lauren would hate to be without her now.

It was then that the name Nicholas Jordan sprang into her mind. Why, she didn't know. Maybe it was the regal manner with which Sheba had left the room. It reminded her of Nicholas's air of self-belief; of utter confidence. Anyway, it certainly hadn't been his car out there in the darkness; she had been able to see that. And why on earth would he be wasting his time watching her in any case? He'd never shown the faintest interest in her, despite their attending the same school in Kingsbridge. Although, to be fair, he'd been a couple of years above her, being that much older, so hadn't really had much contact with her at all.

Nonetheless, she'd developed a bit of a crush on him when one morning she'd seen him striding into school, very much in the manner that Sheba had displayed just moments before. But then ten years ago he'd married the most glamorous girl in the village,

Serena Pemberton, and subsequently left; his aim, so she'd heard (the village possessed an extremely efficient rumour mill), a better and infinitely more prosperous life in London, and that had been the last she'd seen of Nicholas Jordan. Apart from the odd moment or two of nostalgic reflection, she hadn't given him any thought since.

But now out of the blue he was back; had been back for a month or so, in fact: divorced (again this was only rumour) and with a three-year-old daughter, Olivia, in tow.

Lauren hadn't been able to believe her eyes when she'd initially spotted him coming out of the post office-cum-newsagent's; at the time she hadn't heard anything about his return. However, a couple of days after that she'd had cause to visit the newsagent's herself, and a discreet question or two to the owner of the shop, Rosie Turnbull — who prided herself on being the chief information-gatherer of the village — had elicited all of the facts, the main one being how well he'd done in London. He'd been one of the high flyers in banking, according to Rosie, and had made himself a shed load of money — more than enough to purchase Markham Grange, Rosie had gone on to inform her. Markham Grange was the local manor house, and had been the family seat for several generations of the Peckham family. They'd been forced to sell in order to pay ruinous death duties.

Lauren wasn't at all surprised to hear of Nicholas's wealth. After all, hadn't she seen him climbing into a top-of-the-range Jaguar before driving swiftly away? Also, she knew for a fact that the house had been on the market for over two million; she'd seen the details in the local paper.

But it hadn't only been banking that had made him his money, or so Rosie told her. He also owned several companies, bought or taken over in recent years once they'd run into financial trouble. Rosie hinted at a spot of underhand dealing in the process and went on to describe him as 'utterly ruthless, and operating just the right side of the law'. Although how on earth Rosie would know that, Lauren hadn't the faintest idea.

Whatever, he was even more handsome than he'd been as a boy. She smiled wryly to herself now. He'd soon have the local women standing on their heads to attract his attention. Not her, though; she'd long ago got over her girlish crush. She'd had far too much happening in her life to waste time mooning over some boy — or man as he now was, handsome or not.

In fact, she'd been busy making money too; it hadn't only been Nicholas Jordan doing that. Ever since she'd been made redundant five years ago, in fact. She'd made the decision to utilise her redundancy money and make it earn more, so she'd put down a deposit on a run-down, mid-terrace house which was being sold for a ridiculously small sum. She'd spent the next six months repairing and totally refurbishing the property before re-selling it for a very respectable profit. That, along with the low-interest-only mortgage offered to prospective landlords and an unexpected £75,000 inheritance from her grandmother, had been her springboard for an increasingly successful buy-to-let business. She now owned six houses, the rents of which, along with her salary from her day job as PA to the general manager of a local company, provided her with a healthy income, healthy enough to have enabled her to put down a sizable deposit on her own two-bedroom luxury apartment.

All in all, she was a vastly different person to the girl she'd been at school. She'd been known as Ann then, but had since been using her middle name of Lauren, considering it more sophisticated and befitting the professional businesswoman she'd become. In those days she'd been an attractive but studious girl, highly ambitious, and determined to acquire the qualifications needed to forge a profitable career for herself which, to her satisfaction and considerable pride, she had done.

And as far as Nicholas Jordan was concerned, she had no wish to get to know him. Not when she remembered how he'd snubbed her in that final year at school.

A close friend, Fiona, an inveterate matchmaker, had tried to arrange a foursome one evening just months before Nicholas became involved with Serena. Nicholas had been a friend of Fiona's boyfriend, so she'd been confident that he would agree. The plan was that Nicholas would escort Lauren. Only, as Fiona later admitted to Lauren, Nicholas had point-blank refused, saying, 'I don't do blind dates. They're almost always a disaster, and as I haven't a clue who this girl is that you're talking about . . . ' He'd shrugged his shoulders and walked away. He'd had no idea who she was.

She hadn't been surprised by his response, as he only seemed to notice and date the more glamorous girls — and that, she hadn't been. Attractive, yes; glamorous, no. 'His loss' had been her defiant reply to Fiona, and she'd dismissed him from her mind from that moment on. Therefore, taking his taste in girls into account, she hadn't been the least bit surprised to eventually hear that he'd married Serena, who was blonde, extremely lovely, and with a figure to die for.

When Lauren had spotted him for a second time as she'd been leaving the greengrocer's — almost bumped into him, in fact — it was quite evident from the manner in which he regarded her that he still didn't have a clue who she was. Not that she would have expected him to recognise her even if he had known who Fiona had been talking about all those years ago. For gone was the girl she'd been in those days, and in her place was — she hoped — an elegant and sophisticated woman of the world. It was a look she took painstaking care to perfect each and every day, and that morning she'd been particularly pleased with her efforts.

She'd selected a slim grey skirt that finished a couple of inches above her knees and a tailored periwinkle-blue silk blouse over which she wore a three-quarters, figure-hugging jacket. High-heeled grey suede shoes completed her outfit, as well as showing off her shapely legs. She had taken equal care with her makeup, a natural-looking foundation with eyes subtly coloured to emphasize their natural green, and glossy pink lipstick that enhanced the fullness of her lips.

So, not completely unexpectedly, his smile was a warm one, and his eyes gleamed as his glance slid leisurely over her. In fact, he looked as if he was about to speak to her. Lauren didn't allow him the opportunity, however. She simply inclined her head and walked into the next shop along, which just happened to be Jameson's, the butcher's. She couldn't help but notice the look of frustration which crossed Nicholas's face.

Just as she couldn't help smiling to herself as she greeted Tom Jameson. It wasn't unusual for her to call in for a couple of chops and a chat, for Tom was a large, genial man with a ready smile and at times a cheeky sense of humour.

'How're you, love?' he now asked. 'You get more gorgeous each time I see you — which, I have to say, isn't often enough. Sam,' he called then, 'customer.' He glanced back at Lauren. 'Sam will serve you. Get a move on, lad,' he went on. 'The lady hasn't got all day. She only lives over the road, so make sure you treat her properly. Don't want to upset a neighbour, do we?'

'N-no, s-sorry,' the younger man stammered. 'H-how can I-I help you?'

Lauren had glimpsed him in here once or twice but he'd never served her. She'd assumed he was mainly involved in cleaning up and helping with the actual butchery of the meat, somewhere in the hinterland of the shop. Maybe he'd been promoted to sales assistant?

'Two lamb cutlets, please.'

'Certainly.' He indicated two medium-sized cutlets and in a low voice asked, 'Will these do?'

She smiled warmly at him in an attempt to ease his evident shyness, but he kept his gaze fixed on the meat. It was as if he were frightened to look at her.

'Yes, they look perfect. Thank you.'

He did look at her and smiled then — tremulously, it was true, but at least it was a smile, even if it didn't reach his pale eyes. 'I'll just wrap them for you.'

It was unusual for a man of his age — mid- to late twenties, she guessed — to exhibit such diffidence. It was behaviour more appropriate for a teenage boy. With another smile — one that induced a blush upon his fair skin — she turned to leave the shop. Before she could do so, however, she was halted by Tom Jameson calling after her.

'Before you leave, have one of our cards. You can email your order for meat now, and we can have it ready for you to collect on your way home. It's a new service, to appeal to working ladies such as yourself. I know how valuable your time is.' He beamed with pride. 'We're hoping to get a website going in the near future with a proper order form, but till then just email us, saying what you want.'

She glanced at the card he'd given her and, sure enough, it had the phone number and email address printed on it.

'Great, I'll do that.'

Surprisingly, when she got outside once again, Nicholas was only just climbing into his car. Again he glanced her way, with an even more appreciative smile. This time she pretended not to have seen it, and she hadn't given him another thought. Until she'd gone to Fiona's thirtieth birthday party, where who should walk in but Nicholas.

Fiona and Jason had stayed together right from their schooldays and had finally married. As Nicholas had been one of Jason's closest friends, and clearly still was, she should have expected him to be present, she supposed. Not that she'd given him any thought at all. She was well and truly over her absurd infatuation.

Fiona, on the other hand, was thrilled by his arrival. 'Why Nicholas, how lovely,' she'd trilled, clasping both hands to her breast in the manner of a sixteen-year-old girl. 'We didn't think you'd come.' She swivelled and cried, 'Look, Lauren, look who's here. Nicholas, you remember Lauren, don't you? From school?'

Nicholas turned his head and looked at Lauren. Again, admiration glinted at her.

'I'm very glad to meet you, Lauren. I've seen you in the village.' He frowned. 'But, um . . . I don't recall ever meeting you before that, and I'm sure I would have remembered — ' he murmured throatily and provocatively, ' — someone as lovely as you.'

'I called myself Ann in those days. Once I left school I decided to use my middle name — but I'm sure you wouldn't remember me. I don't think we ever actually met.' She stopped there. She wasn't about to tell him that he'd turned down a date with her. He might think she cared.

Instead, she stared at him in silence; at the thick mahogany-coloured hair, the penetrating, slate-grey eyes, the perfectly formed nose, the chiselled jawline, the seductive mouth. He was taller than she remembered, six foot one or two, and definitely more powerfully built. Maturity, she couldn't help but concede, suited him.

His clothes, of course, were designer-made — what else? — and the scent of a very expensive aftershave drifted towards her. Nicholas Jordan had clearly done extremely well for himself with all of his dubious buy-outs and takeovers, and all by the age of — what? Thirty-one, thirty-two?

'So — ' He cocked his head to one side, his gaze narrowing and darkening as if he sensed her hostility. 'Tell me, what do you do?'

'I'm in the buy-to-let business.'

His one eyebrow zoomed upwards. 'Really? How many properties do you own?'

'Six houses to date. I'm in the process of negotiating for the seventh.'

'Good for you. But — ' He frowned. ' — do you make enough to live on from that?'

Despite her resentment that he hadn't made any attempt to hide his surprise at her success, she managed to reply evenly and without rancour. 'Yes, but for now I reinvest the profits I make in more houses. In any case, I retained my day job. I enjoy it too much to give it up. I'm PA to Jonathon Rigsby at Henderson's Engineering. He's the general manager there.'

He studied her intently then, his

interest piqued — that was obvious by his expression. He was about to ask more but Lauren decided she'd told him more than enough — more than she'd intended, in fact — and instead said, 'I hear you've done rather well in London — and you've bought Markham Grange.'

'Yes.' He gave a rueful grimace. 'Although I have to admit I wasn't fully aware of what I was taking on there.'

'Oh?'

'Well the house is a tad run down, shall we say. Even neglected.'

'Didn't you view it before buying? Have a survey done?' She didn't bother trying to conceal her astonishment. But the truth was, she couldn't imagine someone as financially astute as Nicholas must be to have made the sort of money he had buying blindly, especially not in the case of a house; and a house, moreover, which had probably cost him upwards of two million pounds.

'I did, but the owners had done a splendid job of hiding the exact state of it all and I was in such a hurry to buy it that I accepted everything at face value. Stupid, I know, but I so wanted to get back here. It's always been where I've felt most at home.'

Lauren almost laughed at that remark. She'd have put money on his feeling totally at home in London amongst all the other wealthy bankers. A sleepy village was the last place she'd have imagined him preferring. However, she didn't say anything. And she could hardly agree with him on his other point — that he had, in fact, been stupid.

'Still,' he went on, 'I've hired a very reputable firm of renovators, so they'll soon knock it into shape, I'm sure.'

Yes, she decided, she was sure they would. He wouldn't want to get his own hands dirty. Not like her, who'd carried out a lot of the work herself on the properties she'd invested in. Still, to be fair, if she could have afforded to hire tradesmen to do it, she probably would have.

She thought then of her closest friend, Stella, who owned the hairdressing salon beneath Lauren's flat. She'd originally worked for a business which Nicholas had bought a couple of years ago when it had hit the financial skids. Within a week, he'd instructed one of his people to walk in and inform a good half of the employees that they were being made redundant, one of whom had been Stella. He hadn't even had the decency to do it himself, she'd grumbled at the time. In his defence, he'd still been living in London then — so maybe it hadn't been easy for him to be the one to give the workforce news of the loss of their jobs.

However, as Stella liked to point out, the redundancy money had been enough to enable her to put down a deposit on her salon — something she'd always hoped to own — so it hadn't all been bad. But as Stella had said at the time, Nicholas hadn't seemed to give a toss about what would happen to the people he was getting rid of, and what had made it even worse was that he still hadn't put in an appearance by the time they all left for good. Clearly, all he was concerned with were the future profits of the streamlined company.

'I'm sure they will,' she retorted waspishly. 'After all, money buys most things, doesn't it? Even people's jobs.' And she stared directly at him as she said those words. He couldn't have failed to get her meaning — that money meant more to him than people's livelihoods.

He didn't respond to that comment, however. Instead, he tilted his head to one side and allowed his gaze to move, deliberately slowly it seemed, over her heart-shaped face with its jade-green eyes, pert nose, and rose-tinted mouth, a face that was attractively framed by an abundance of naturally toffee-coloured and gold-streaked hair — hair that no matter what she did, simply went its own wild way, as it had done this evening. In an effort to match the elegance of her outfit, she'd wound it up in a topknot of sorts, but slowly, inexorably, several long strands were working themselves free and falling in a curly cascade around her ears. His gaze lingered on the wayward locks before sliding on down over her body, pausing momentarily on the rounded breasts that her low-cut dress daringly revealed; breasts that in Lauren's opinion would benefit from a bit more fullness but which, judging by the glint that reappeared in Nicholas's eyes, pleased him.

All of a sudden, Lauren had an almost irresistible urge to cover as much as she could of herself with her hands. In fact, she was sorely tempted to ask him whether he knew it was rude to stare. However, she decided better of it and said nothing. Instead, she demanded of herself, why hadn't she worn something that would have provided a bit of camouflage — like a nun's habit, for instance — instead of this figure-hugging dress that accentuated each one of her curves?

'It most assuredly does,' he smoothly drawled. 'Do you have a problem with that, Lauren? After all, you must have employed people to work in your houses. Or were they already in a fit state to rent?'

'Some were, more or less, but a lot of the work I did myself in the evenings and weekends. It was a steep learning curve but it kept my costs down.' She shrugged as if it had all been easy, when it had actually been extremely hard. She'd made more than one mistake in the beginning, but she'd persevered so that now she could take pride in being reasonably expert in the field of DIY. She'd even decorated her own flat just recently. 'Anyway, it's entirely up to you what you do with your money.'

'Quite,' he murmured, the admiration fading from his eyes as his expression hardened and his mouth tightened with exasperation at her perceived criticism of him. 'And let's not forget that I'm employing local craftsmen in the process and putting money into their coffers. Which, quite obviously, you have failed to do.'

Now it was her turn to feel exasperated. She nibbled at her bottom lip, a gesture that had his glance moving to and lingering on her full lips. So intense was his gaze that she felt as if he were touching her. A tiny flame ignited deep in her stomach. Dear God, she couldn't still be attracted to him — could she? That was the last thing she needed. As a result of her dismay, her next words erupted rather more harshly than she'd intended. 'I just hope that a centuries-old house isn't ruined and over-modernised in the process.'

'It won't be,' he bit out, equally as harshly. 'I'm as keen as you obviously are to preserve our heritage.' He suddenly reached out and brushed her one shoulder with his hand. 'I'll just get rid of that rather large chip that you seem to delight in flaunting.'

Lauren stared at him, unable to believe what he'd just done and said.

'Well,' she heatedly snapped, 'I'll relieve you of my company in that case.' She swivelled smartly around to walk away from him, seething with anger. She'd poke both her eyes out with a cocktail stick and cut off her tongue before she'd bother speaking to him again. Maybe she should be grateful that he'd refused the blind date all those years ago. How could she have had a crush on someone like him? Of course she'd never actually spoken to him at the time, and so couldn't have known anything about his character. Well she knew now, and she vowed there and then to steer well clear of him. One thing was obvious, at any rate: the postmistress, Rosie, had been spot-on in her description of him. Not only was he totally ruthless, but he was also revoltingly arrogant and cruelly sarcastic into the bargain.

It was one thing to decide to banish Nicholas Jordan from her head, but it was quite another to do it, and maddeningly, her enjoyment of the party went downhill from that moment. Because wherever she looked, there he was, smiling mockingly at her; delighting, she suspected, in irritating her.

It took the arrival of Greg Mallory to lighten her increasingly black mood. She'd always liked Greg. He, too, had been at school with her; in her class, actually. He'd been friendly, even-tempered, amusing — the complete antithesis to Nicholas. Even his looks had been cast into the shade by the older boy. Fair where Nicholas was dark, and lighter in build, he'd also been four or five inches shorter. He'd grown since then but he still wasn't as tall as Nicholas.

His blue eyes beamed out at Lauren now from beneath his dishevelled dark blond hair. They'd dated for a while after they'd both left school but it hadn't worked out, at least not for her, and they'd decided to end things. She'd suspected that Greg's feelings for her went much deeper, however, and he would have willingly — even enthusiastically — carried on their relationship.

'Hi, Greg,' she greeted him now, unable to hide her relief at any sort of distraction from the sensation of Nicholas's eyes boring into her. 'I haven't seen you in a while — well, in quite a while actually. How are things?'

'Oh, you know — busy, busy. Always working.'

'Tell me about it. You look well.' And he did; he also looked more handsome than she remembered. She felt a piercing of attraction as well as nostalgia for their days as a couple. 'How's your brother, by the way — Paul, isn't it? I haven't glimpsed him either.' Paul was Greg's twin. 'You used to always be together at school; never saw one without the other,' she joked. 'I half expected you to go on and work together.'

'No, he went to America, New York, to work for one of the big banks.' Good grief, she mused, yet another banker. Was there no escaping them? 'It didn't work out. He's just returned, actually, and is trying, unsuccessfully, to find a job.' He grimaced wryly.

'Are you still alike?' she asked. 'I often recall the terrible tricks you played on us all at school. We never knew who was who of the pair of you. It caused mayhem on more than one occasion,' she laughed.

Greg glanced around. 'See for yourself. He's here somewhere. Oh, there he is — over there.' He pointed to a man, a man who still bore a marked similarity to Greg. He was talking animatedly to another man whom Lauren didn't recognise.

As if Paul sensed he was being watched, he swivelled his head and looked across the room at his brother and Lauren. He didn't seem to know her straight away but then she saw the penny drop and he smiled. Lauren mouthed 'Hi' before turning back to Greg.

'Yes — you're still very much alike.'

The only way she'd been able to tell

them apart in their schooldays was by checking one of Paul's index fingers — the one on his left hand, if she remembered rightly. He'd cut himself with a pen-knife he'd been messing around with, deeply enough to leave a scar. She'd actually seen him do it and after that, whenever the two of them had played one of their pranks, that had always been what she'd looked for. It had been the only way then to tell them apart.

She glanced back at Paul, but he looked wholly engaged in conversation with the same man and didn't seem to notice her looking at him. He'd been a difficult boy, as she recalled, prone to switching from exuberantly high spirits to what she supposed could be termed teenage angst, unlike Greg who'd always been the same: charmingly amiable. However, from the look of Paul now — smiling, chatting good-naturedly — maturity had smoothed those flaws out and he looked every bit as likable as his brother.

Mind you, for all his engaging charm, it had been Greg who'd usually instigated the pranks. Paul had simply followed his lead. Greg had always maintained that was because he was the older twin by five minutes and so was five minutes smarter, which sounded quite ridiculous; but he had undoubtedly been the cleverer of the two, always ahead of his brother in the exam results. Still, it hadn't seemed to worry Paul.

'I've been hearing a few rumours about you,' he drawled. 'People are saying you're on your way to making a fortune.'

'I wish,' she laughed.

'So tell me about the buy-to-let business. It is that that you're involved in, isn't it? Or have I misunderstood?'

'No, that's right, but I still work at Henderson's.'

'That must keep you busy. How do you manage to juggle the two separate things?'

'With difficulty sometimes, but I

manage. I've only got six houses at the moment.'

'Only!' he exclaimed with a wry smile. 'That's impressive in my opinion. Tell me, is it profitable?'

Nicholas had asked the same question. Did all men think firstly about the money one could make from something? Mind you, she mused, was she really any different? She wouldn't be working herself so hard if it wasn't worthwhile financially.

'Reasonable. I need to hang on to my day job, though.' Again she laughed.

Greg eyed her keenly then. 'I hear you've just had a bit of a contretemps with our resident millionaire. A word to the wise — don't let him trample all over you. Because I'm sure he will if you give him half a chance. Always liked to be the one in control, did Jordan, if I recall things correctly from school. I couldn't stand him then either.'

Lauren groaned. 'The gossip mill's up to speed then?'

'It sure is. So tell me every detail about what happened.'

'Well, I had the sheer effrontery to express my fears about what he's doing — or might be about to do — to that house.'

'You didn't!' He burst into laughter.

'I did, I'm afraid, and he didn't appreciate my honesty.' She pulled a face. 'He accused me of having a chip on my shoulder.'

'Did he? I can't imagine that went down well.'

'It didn't, take it from me.' She glanced over at Nicholas, but this time he wasn't looking her way. He was much too involved with the attractive blonde at his side.

She wasn't surprised; he'd always made a beeline for the prettiest girls, one of whom had been Serena. It hadn't done him much good, though, seeing as how they'd ended up divorced.

'Oh dear,' Greg was murmuring. 'You've blotted your copybook then.'

She raised an enquiring eyebrow at this.

'Well, I have heard that he's a bit sensitive about having bought such a white elephant. Doesn't like people thinking he's less than perfect.'

'Well, really,' she snorted, yet again glancing across at Nicholas, 'for a man who's supposed to be so damned smart . . . '

'I know. Unbelievable, isn't it?' Greg's voice was steadily rising, making Lauren wonder how much he'd had to drink. As he'd only just arrived at the party, he must have had a few beforehand. 'Still, he's got enough money to throw a good chunk of it around.' He gave another loud laugh. Several heads turned, one of which happened to be Nicholas's. He looked straight at Lauren, his expression hardening with what looked remarkably like disapproval.

Stung by this, she defiantly returned his stare before turning her gaze back to Greg.

'You'll have to stop looking at him,' Greg bluntly told her. 'People might start to think you fancy him.'

'Huh! I'd as soon fancy a rattle-snake.'

'Glad to hear it,' was Greg's response. 'Look, how about we leave. I'll take you home, or we could go and have a drink somewhere. Do a bit of catching up. You clearly aren't enjoying yourself any more than I am.'

His gaze was a warm one now — a bit too warm, making Lauren wonder if he was hoping to take up where they'd left off eleven years ago. She liked Greg but that was all it was; liking. Just as it had been all that time ago if she was honest. She'd never felt passion for him. In fact, there'd been very few men who had inspired that emotion. Which was why she was still alone with only a cat for company at night.

'You're right there,' she told him, 'but I can get myself back. I've brought my car.'

'Suit yourself.'

His tone was an unexpectedly sulky one. The good humour was gone; clearly she'd managed to upset him as well. That had to be some sort of personal best. She'd succeeded in upsetting two men in a little over ten minutes. In Greg's case, however, she made an effort to placate him. 'I'm sorry, but I really can't leave yet. Fiona would be hurt, but you go if you want.'

'I think I will. I can't bear to watch everybody bowing and scraping to Jordan for another second.' He swung and walked away, leaving Lauren staring after him.

'Well, I hope he wasn't including me in that last remark,' she murmured to herself.

But now, just a week later, she asked herself, had she really upset Nicholas enough that evening with her remarks to induce him to set up some sort of watch on her flat? In an effort, maybe, to inflict some sort of macabre punishment by trying to frighten her? Could he really be that controlling?

That vindictive? She sighed. Greg had seemed to think so — at least, about the controlling bit. He really did dislike Nicholas, almost as much as she did. She wondered if the two of them had had some sort of run-in.

Still, as much as she disliked Nicholas, she found it hard to believe it could be him behind what was going on. Mainly because she couldn't imagine that he'd waste his time on such an activity, or that he'd care enough about her opinion of him. Unless — could he have paid someone else to do it? Someone from the murky underworld? If, as Rosie had suggested, he conducted his business just the right side of legal, he'd most likely know the appropriate people for the job. And it would explain the car not being his. But would he stoop that low? And, looked at rationally, would he even have bothered giving her a second's thought in the aftermath of the party, given that he'd seemed to be getting on so well with the attractive blonde?

It seemed highly unlikely, so it had to be someone else — if, indeed, the surveillance was targeted at her. And the truth was, she wasn't even sure about that. Maybe she was imagining trouble where there was none.

Yet, for all her sensible reasoning, it did seem a bit of a coincidence that she should have first noticed the car in the wake of the party and her and Nicholas's disagreement.

2

But if she'd decided Nicholas wouldn't have given her another second's thought, maddeningly, she couldn't seem to stop thinking about him. Mainly, she reasoned, because she saw him everywhere she went: driving through the village; walking with a small girl, his daughter presumably; coming out of local shops. Each time, he made a point of acknowledging her: a wave from his car; a smiling glance from the other side of the street; and finally, coming to a halt directly in front of her, along with his daughter, effectively blocking her progress along the pavement.

He bent his head and looked down at the little girl at his side, his expression softening as he said, 'Olivia, this is Lauren.' He glanced back at Lauren, his expression changing to one of challenge almost; it was as if he were daring her to somehow get round them and walk on by. 'Lauren, my daughter, Olivia.'

'Hello, Lauren,' the small girl said, holding out a tiny hand as she did so. 'I'm pleased to meet you.'

Lauren smiled down at her, leaning forward so that her head was almost on a level with the child's. Olivia dimpled at her. She was adorable. Pity the same couldn't be said of her father. 'Hello, Olivia. I'm very pleased to meet you too.'

The girl cocked her head and asked, 'Are you a friend of my daddy's?'

Completely stumped by that, Lauren failed to come up with any sort of answer. It was Nicholas who responded.

'She soon will be, I hope.'

His smile now was a provocative one. He'd guessed what she was thinking — that she would never be a friend of his. In fact, she was tempted to confirm that by telling him that hell would have to become a desirable holiday destination before that would happen. She hadn't forgotten — or forgiven — his insulting action at Fiona's party even if he had. Of course she didn't say anything of the sort, even though her fingers were itching to swipe the smile away. She wondered how he'd react if she succumbed to her urge. Probably hit her back. Yet if she were totally honest, she simply couldn't imagine Nicholas Jordan hitting anyone, let alone a woman.

'You'll have to come to tea,' Olivia said in a quaintly old-fashioned tone.

'What a good idea.' Nicholas readily — eagerly, in fact — endorsed his daughter's invitation. 'How about tomorrow when you finish work?'

Lauren stared at him. He couldn't be serious. Tea, for heaven's sake? The very notion of Nicholas sitting down to a traditional afternoon tea was a farcical one. As farcical as the idea of her actually going. She almost burst out laughing, right there and then. She would have but for the fact that her mind was frantically searching for a credible reason to refuse, because there was no way she was going to take tea with Nicholas Jordan. She'd rather chew her own arm off. 'Um, well . . . '

'Oh ple-ease,' Olivia beseeched her, gazing up at Lauren from wide blue eyes and clasping her two little hands to her chest as she hopped from one foot to the other. 'You can meet Fern.'

'Fern?' Did the poor child have to make do with a plant as a substitute for a friend?

'Yes, my nanny.'

'Oh, I see. Well — '

'Please come,' Nicholas murmured. 'Don't disappoint her. I can see she's taken to you and it will give me the chance to make up for my incivility of the other evening.'

Lauren stared at him. How could he use his lovable small daughter to get his own way? Was there nothing he wouldn't stoop to? However, his underhand tactic gained him a definitive win in the battle of wills, because she found it impossible to refuse. How could she disappoint Olivia, even though everything within her was warning her not to give way to this man's persuasions? She looked down at the little girl; the small face was alight with anticipation. So although her every instinct was screaming, 'Don't do it,' she heard herself saying, 'Of course, I'd love to come.' So much for preferring to chew her own arm off to taking afternoon tea with Nicholas Jordan.

She did, however, make a point of smiling solely at Olivia. It was only a small gesture of rebellion but it did go some way towards helping to minimise her feeling of defeat. Even so, she sensed his satisfaction at her agreement. It was very much against her better judgement that she finally slanted a glance at him, only to have him mouth a silent 'thank you' to her. Well, at least he had the grace to show some gratitude.

As for Olivia, she quickened her skipping on the spot. 'Oh, goody.' She clapped her hands. 'Now, what do you like to eat?'

Lauren couldn't help but grin. Who could possibly refuse her? Not Lauren. She was curious as to where the child had learnt such charm. From her mother? From what she recalled of her, she wouldn't imagine so. Serena had always been thoroughly modern; thoroughly self-centred. Lauren wondered then where she was and how often she saw her daughter. Because it looked as if Olivia lived with her father.

'Well now, let me see.' She pretended to give the matter some serious thought. 'I love egg and cress sandwiches, and maybe a cake?'

She glanced at Nicholas and encountered a gaze that was warm with approval — and something else. What that something else was, however, she found it impossible to fathom.

'That's settled then,' he said. 'What time shall we expect you?'

'Oh, five thirty-ish, quarter to six. I'll have to go home and feed my cat first.

That's her teatime too,' she told Olivia, 'and she'll be very angry if she doesn't get it. In fact, she probably won't speak to me all evening.'

Olivia chuckled. 'Cats don't speak, they meow.'

'Well, this one almost speaks. I certainly know what she's trying to say.'

Olivia clapped her hands. 'Can I come and see her sometime? I love cats. Mummy wouldn't let me have one.' Her little face saddened.

'Of course you can. She'd love to see you, I'm sure. She adores little girls.' Lauren had no idea whether she did or not. All she could do was offer up a silent prayer that she would be proved right and that Sheba didn't behave in her customary stroppy manner with anyone she didn't know. 'It's just men she can't stand.' She couldn't help herself; she glanced pointedly at Nicholas, only to be greeted with a quizzical stare. 'She was very badly treated by a teenage boy.'

'Oh, I see,' he murmured. 'I was

about to say like mistress, like cat.'

She ignored that — it wasn't worthy of any sort of response — and swept her gaze back to Olivia. 'Someday soon, eh?'

'Oh, yes please.'

'Anyway, five thirty-ish will be perfect,' Nicholas told her. 'I'll have finished for the day by that time. We'll see you then.' Holding Olivia by the hand, he walked away from her, Olivia still chattering excitedly — 'Imagine Daddy, she has a cat!' — at the same time waving over her shoulder to Lauren.

A pang of sympathy for the little girl pierced her at the awful image of having Nicholas Jordan for a father and Serena for a mother. She didn't know which was the worse prospect. Yet to be fair, Nicholas had looked very fond of his daughter, and only too ready to indulge her with whatever she wished for. In this instance, tea with Lauren. It couldn't be something he'd be accustomed to doing — or even really wanted to do, she was sure.

A piercing of envy stirred within her. Such affection was something she'd always longed for but never had. For Alex, her father, was a cold, unemotional man. She couldn't remember him ever hugging her, telling her he loved her, reading her a bedtime story; he was far too wrapped up in himself. Her mother had tried to compensate for his deficiencies by being extra caring and attentive, but nothing could replace the love of a man for his child — the sort of love she'd just witnessed, in fact. She'd often wondered if his lack of any sort of natural paternal emotion was down to them not having Lauren until they were in their early forties — certainly in her father's case. He'd remarked more than once that having a child had changed their lives almost beyond recognition and it hadn't been said with any discernible degree of pleasure. In fact, Lauren had wondered whether he'd have preferred not to have a child. They'd been retired now for some years and were living on the south coast of Cornwall. Lauren tried to visit them, but it didn't happen as regularly as she would have liked. Needless to say, her parents never visited her; and that, she suspected, was down entirely to her father.

* * *

Throughout the whole of the following day, she found herself irritably wondering what had possessed her to consent to a visit to Markham Grange. Other than not wanting to disappoint a small girl, that was.

Nicholas would clearly be there, having told her he'd be finished with work for the day by then, which led her to wonder what on earth they would find to talk about. Surely they'd have nothing in common. He was a wealthy banker, while she — well, she supposed she hadn't done too badly for herself, but if she compared her success with Nicholas's, hers looked extremely paltry. Still, hopefully Olivia's chatter would fill any awkward silences. And despite her reluctance to go, it would provide her with the opportunity to view what had been done so far to the interior of the house — or at least the small part of it that she'd see. She couldn't imagine he'd go the lengths of showing her around, not after her disparaging comments at the party.

She'd told Stella the evening before what she'd agreed to when she'd popped into the salon on her way back to her flat. Her friend's initial greeting had been a cool, 'Well hi, stranger. Too busy these days to call in?'

'Sorry, life has been a bit hectic.'

'I never seem to see you anymore. You're too busy; too tired to go for a drink. You haven't got that many friends that you can afford to lose me,' she'd waspishly pointed out, blue eyes flashing as she did so.

Lauren stared at her friend. She'd always envied Stella her hourglass figure, at times longing for the same sort of voluptuous curves, as hers seemed very modest in comparison. She didn't envy her the occasionally fiery temper, however, or her brutally frank way of speaking. Still, it went with the auburn hair, she supposed, and she should be used to it by this time. 'You're right, I'll make more of an effort.'

Stella snorted. 'If it's that much of an effort, don't bother.'

'I didn't mean that. Come on, Stell, you're my oldest friend. We've always been more like sisters, haven't we?' She felt bad about neglecting her but the truth was, she'd had a lot to preoccupy her lately — not least the suspicion that she was being stalked. She wondered if she should tell Stella, but would that just make it all the more plausible? More real? She decided to hold her horses and wait and see what happened. It might just peter out, in which case she'd have been worrying for no good reason. 'Let's meet for a drink at the Frog tomorrow evening. I've got to take tea first at Markham Grange.'

Stella gasped. 'You what?'

'I've been invited for tea.'

'You're kidding me,' Stella had cried, her annoyance with Lauren instantly forgotten — for the moment at least, although Lauren's neglect of her would probably be brought up again at some point. Stella could hold a grudge for days — weeks, even. It was her chief flaw in Lauren's opinion, and it had caused many a disagreement between them in the past. They always made up again, but it left a slightly sour taste afterwards as far as Lauren was concerned. 'You're going to take tea with Nicholas Jordan?' She hooted with laughter. 'A more unlikely scenario than that one, I can't imagine.'

'I know.' Lauren grimaced wryly. 'I can't believe I agreed.'

'Have you taken leave of your senses?'

'I must have,' she sighed.

'From all I've heard — and, of

course, from personal experience, although I haven't actually met him — I have to say the man's a predator,' Stella cried. 'He'll eat you alive.'

'Between two slices of bread no doubt.'

'I wouldn't be at all surprised.' Stella eyed her more seriously then. 'You know he has his daughter living with him?'

'Yes. It was Olivia who actually invited me.'

'Really?'

'Yeah. She's a little sweetie and the main reason I said I'd go. Those bewitching blue eyes — I felt I couldn't disappoint her. Um, changing the subject, sort of. Where's Serena, do you know?'

'Went off with some other bloke, or so I heard. Someone even richer than Nicholas by all accounts.'

'Wow! Mind you, I seem to recall she always did have an eye to the main chance. How long have she and Nicholas been divorced?'

'Haven't a clue.' Stella eyed her once more. 'What's with this sudden interest? You don't fancy your chances, do you?'

'Are you kidding? I'm only going because Olivia was so keen for me to. Do you know, I think the poor little thing's lonely, and she must miss her mother. How could any woman leave her child — her only child, at that? Of course, I don't know if that's what happened. Maybe it's just a temporary arrangement, living with her father.'

'Again — ' Stella shrugged. ' — haven't a clue.'

'I'm hoping it will just be me, Olivia, and the nanny, Fern.'

'Fern?' Stella exclaimed. 'A pretty fancy name for a nanny. I say.' Her eyes sparkled with excited speculation. 'She's not Nicholas's bit on the side, is she? You know, masquerading as a nanny?'

'How would I know?' But maybe Stella had hit the nail on the head. In which case, why was he showing interest in Lauren? Or had she imagined it all?

* * *

Five o'clock swiftly came round and it was time to leave work. As Lauren had told Olivia, she had to go home first and feed Sheba before going to the Grange. Her pet greeted her in her usual manner by winding herself around Lauren's legs, meowing loudly as she did so. 'Yes, okay, let me get to the cupboard and I'll feed you.' As if the animal had understood, she freed Lauren and Lauren pulled out a tin of her favourite food and spooned it into her bowl.

She lowered the bowl to the tiled floor before straightening up and glancing round her recently fitted kitchen. She was extremely proud of what she'd done here. The flat was a large one, stretching across two of the shops below. It included a spacious sitting room which she'd furnished comfortably with two squashy settees and an armchair. She'd splurged out on a flat-screen television with all the attachments: a digi-box and DVD player, as well as a good sound system and CD player. Her bedroom, one of two, was also spacious; spacious enough to accommodate a stylish black-and-white tiled en-suite shower room and toilet. There was another bathroom, also luxuriously tiled in aqua and ivory tiles, as well as a generously sized jacuzzi bath and power shower.

She sighed with pleasure. Her hard work at school had finally paid off. She had the expertise to manage her own business affairs without having to call and pay for the services of an accountant. She'd discovered she was also an excellent negotiator when it came to buying the houses.

She glanced down at her cat, murmuring, 'Okay, now I'm going out for a while.'

The cat lifted her head, emitting another meow — this time in what sounded like a protest — before she lowered her head again and concentrated on finishing her dinner. Lauren eventually let herself out of her flat and began to make her way to Markham Grange. It was close enough to walk to, as was her place of work. In fact, the three destinations were all within fairly easy reach of each other. On a fine morning she often walked to work, as she had today, the weather for mid-October being textbook-perfect. An early low-lying mist had swiftly been dispersed by the power of the rising sun, which had in turn enhanced the autumn colours, clothing the trees and hedgerows in a blaze of red, gold, and bronze. The scent of wood smoke wafted towards her on the breeze from the chimney of a nearby cottage. It all made for a breathtakingly beautiful scene and had provided the perfect start to her working day.

Nicholas's house, as she reached it now, was equally breathtaking. Three storeys and constructed of rose-red brick, it sported row upon row of mullioned windows, their small glass panes glinting diamond-bright in the late sunshine, and it all sat beneath a grey slate, steeply sloping roof. It made her flat look pretty small in comparison. She walked across the vast gravelled forecourt to an imposing front door — oak with an attractive fanlight above it — and rang the bell. Almost at once she heard the sound of running feet, and the door was flung open to reveal Olivia standing alongside a young woman whom she assumed was Fern.

'You must be Lauren,' the woman said. 'I've heard so much about you from Olivia,' she laughed. 'I feel I already know you. She's so excited. But please, come in. Nicholas is waiting for us in the drawing room.'

So he was here. She'd been hoping he wouldn't be; that something would have urgently demanded his attention, preferably somewhere else — something like another business to buy and more staff to make redundant. It wasn't to be. Sadly, he was still here. She had no option but to follow the woman and child inside, Olivia immediately taking her hand.

'I'm so pleased to see you,' the little girl told her with a skip of pure pleasure.

'And I'm pleased to see you,' Lauren replied with a grin. And she genuinely was, she realised.

With Olivia still hanging onto her hand, Lauren followed Fern into a room that was sufficiently elegant to grace the glossy pages of a country house magazine. It was a perfect example of Regency splendour, all done out in eggshell blue, the palest pink and ivory, with deeply cushioned cream settees and chairs, elegant antique tables and cabinets, and what looked like genuine old master paintings hanging on the walls. Heavy silk curtains hung at the windows, luxuriant enough to puddle on the floor. Clearly no expense had been spared in the renovation; and what was more, it had been executed with faultless taste. Once again, it cast her flat into the shade.

Nicholas, of course, had noticed her keen glances around and his expression when she finally looked at him was surprisingly apprehensive.

'I hope it meets with your approval,' he quietly said.

'It does,' she admitted somewhat grudgingly. Then, unable to help herself, she went on, 'It's gorgeous, actually.'

'Good.' Nicholas allowed himself another smile; a distinctly satisfied one this time before inviting her to sit down. He indicated one of the armchairs. 'Mrs Hodges is about to bring the tea in.'

'I'll go and give her a hand,' Fern offered, and promptly exited the room.

Lauren's heart took a nosedive. The last thing she'd wanted was to be left alone with Nicholas. Thank goodness for Olivia and her seamless stream of chatter; it effectively masked any awkward silences between herself and her host. She seated herself in the chair that Nicholas had waved her to and immediately sank down by a good six inches into the incredibly soft cushions. Olivia went to the settee, still talking excitedly, and Nicholas took the chair opposite Lauren — which instantly made Lauren feel uneasy. She really didn't want to be the object of his scrutiny while she took tea. She was bound to drip or spill something. Not that she was usually clumsy, but she suspected, under the present circumstances, that she might well be. Nicholas Jordan seemed to have the knack of disturbing her customary composure.

A low table sat between them all upon which the woman who now entered the room, and whom she presumed was the housekeeper, set the large tray. It held several plates of sandwiches and three different sorts of cake. Fern brought up the rear with another tray upon which sat all that was needed for cups of tea. The two women removed everything from the trays, the paraphernalia covering the entire table top.

'Fern, can you be mother?' Nicholas asked.

Mrs Hodges had left the room again. Thank goodness Fern was staying. She couldn't imagine what sort of conversation she and Nicholas would conduct if left alone. Because sooner or later Olivia was bound to run out of steam — although there was no sign of that so far. Lauren couldn't help thinking, however, that the nanny's presence did seem to suggest that Stella's remark about Fern being Nicholas's 'bit on the side' might have some foundation to it.

Lauren took the delicate porcelain cup and saucer from the young woman. Olivia was handed a glass of milk.

'There are egg and cress sandwiches,' the little girl gleefully told her.

'How lovely,' Lauren enthused, taking the utmost care to avoid Nicholas's eyes. Just as she'd feared, they didn't seem to have left her from the time she'd walked into the room and, as a result, she was aware of the faintest of blushes tingeing her cheeks. Good grief, she never blushed. What on earth was wrong with her? Nonetheless, she politely took just one of the small, neatly cut triangular sandwiches.

'Take several,' Nicholas bade her. 'They are rather tiny. Mrs Hodges' notion of tea fit for the aristocracy.' He grinned.

'I hope you told her I wasn't one of them,' she smartly said, doing as he'd instructed and helping herself to three more.

The food turned out to be absolutely delicious and Lauren found herself sampling some of everything on the table, even going back for second portions of some of it. 'Mmm,' she eventually sighed, placing her empty plate onto the table top, 'that was gorgeous.'

'I do love a woman who enjoys her food,' Nicholas remarked, his eyes gleaming as they skimmed over what was left on the plates — which, it had to be said, wasn't a lot.

The flush revisited Lauren's cheeks. Maybe it was warm in here and that was what was responsible for her blushes? Or was it the fact that he seemed to be insinuating that she was greedy? 'It was all so tasty,' she excused herself. 'It would be a shame not to enjoy it.'

'No, I meant it. I wasn't being rude. So many women decline anything which might be fattening and in my view they miss out on one of the greatest treats in life: good food. It's refreshing to meet one who genuinely relishes eating.'

Could he be talking about Serena? She had been the fortunate possessor of the sort of figure other women would be prepared to die for; to keep it that way she must have had to be strict with her diet.

Proving her right, Olivia said, 'Mummy didn't eat cake, did she, Daddy?'

'No,' was all Nicholas murmured, however.

Lauren glanced out of the window at that point and, to her dismay, saw that the light was fading fast. She'd have to walk along a fairly lonely stretch of lane to reach the village, which hadn't bothered her on the way here. However, as it was now nearing six thirty and the lane was heavily tree-lined, as well as there being no lighting of any sort, she'd be walking back in complete darkness.

A stabbing of unease pierced her as she recalled the sight of the car parked outside her flat several nights running with its unrecognisable occupant. Who was to say that he wasn't watching her all the time and so knew exactly where she was? He could even be out there somewhere . . .

'I'd better go.' She sprang to her feet. 'I hadn't realised the time. It must be Olivia's bedtime.'

'Did you drive here?' Nicholas unexpectedly asked.

'No, I walked. It's not far, so it didn't seem worth using the car.'

'Where do you live? I'll drive you back.'

Fern had also got to her feet by this time and was busily stacking the dishes back onto the trays. She hadn't spoken much throughout, other than to say a few things quietly to Olivia. Which belatedly made Lauren doubt the validity of Stella's guesswork about a relationship between her and Nicholas. If there was something going on, wouldn't she have joined in the conversation? Because let's face it, there'd been ample opportunity. Conversation between Nicholas and his guest hadn't exactly flowed; but for Olivia there would have been even longer and infinitely more embarrassing silences. Although the little girl did seem to have finally exhausted her extensive repertoire.

'No, really, it isn't far.' The last thing she wanted was to have to sit alongside Nicholas Jordan in the enforced intimacy of a vehicle. 'I'll be fine.' She glanced again through the window. It was getting darker with every moment that passed. A flicker of something — fear? — made itself felt; it was certainly considerably stronger than simple unease.

Nicholas frowned. Had he sensed her urgent desire to leave; her apprehension? 'I insist. It's too dark for you to walk alone.'

She couldn't argue with that. Fortunately, as she'd said, it wasn't far; a five-minute drive, if that, in his Jaguar.

She needn't have worried, however, as the journey was over almost before it had begun. It wasn't until he brought the car to a standstill in front of her flat that he finally spoke.

'Thank you for indulging Olivia. I really appreciate it.'

She'd been on the point of opening the door and climbing from the front passenger seat when his words halted her. Out of politeness she swung back to face him, although she'd much rather have left right there and then. She'd felt uncomfortable in his company, on edge, mainly because her old feelings of attraction to him were — unbelievably — resurrecting themselves. Her pulses had quickened at his proximity, as had her heartbeat. And there she'd been, supremely confident that she'd got over all that silliness years ago.

'She doesn't see many people. I've been thinking of getting her into some sort of nursery group in preparation for school eventually. It would also give her the opportunity to make friends. Is there a good one in the village, do you know?'

Why would he think she'd know such a thing? She didn't have children. Nonetheless, she gave the question some thought and then said, 'I believe Vera Smith runs one, but how good it is I couldn't say, not having any children.' She smiled lamely at him. 'You could ask Rosie Turnbull in the post office. She knows practically everything that goes on in the village.'

'Ye-es.' He grinned ruefully. 'I'm beginning to realise that. Did she always live here and run the post office? I don't recall her from my school days.'

'No, she arrived after you left, but it didn't take her long to become au fait with all that happens in the village.' She found herself grinning back at him. 'It seems to be a particular talent of hers, unearthing the news about everyone. Some might even presume to call it gossip.'

He laughed. 'Right, I'll be sure to bear that in mind in future.' He then proceeded to scrutinise her for a moment or two before saying, 'I'm surprised you're not married, with your own family. I noticed you're not wearing a wedding ring,' he added — in response, she presumed, to her quizzical look.

'No, I'm not.'

'Why not?' he bluntly asked. 'The men around here blind or something?'

Her heartbeat once again accelerated.

Did his words mean he found her attractive? 'Not as far as I know.' Somehow — she had no idea how — her voice remained steady; cool, even.

'So, how have you escaped the marital state this long?' His head was tilted to one side as he studied her from beneath lowered eyelids.

She shrugged. 'It's not a question of escaping anything, or anyone. I've never met anyone I could envisage spending the rest of my life with.'

He continued to scrutinise her. Lauren began to feel . . . well, fidgety she supposed was the best way to describe it. The conversation was becoming far too personal for comfort.

'You and Greg Mallory seemed to be getting on well the other evening.'

'Yes we were, but I can't say I've ever viewed him as potential husband material. Don't get me wrong. He's a lovely guy, just not for me.'

He eyed her curiously now. 'What sort of . . . guy are you looking for?'

Someone like you were the words

that sprang into her head. Dear Lord! Where had that come from? Nicholas was the very last man she'd want to be married to. She was quite sure he'd expect to be the boss in any relationship and that was something she'd never be able to endure. She was way too independent; too accustomed to making her own decisions.

'I'm not really sure.'

'Are you not?' He quirked an eyebrow at her. 'It sounds to me as if you've got it all worked out.'

She met his gaze defiantly. 'Someone considerate, I suppose; loyal, kind, loving. He must have ambition . . . ' Her words trailed off. She'd spotted the gleam within his eye. Oh God. Now what was coming? She'd begun to know him well enough to know what that something was.

He didn't disappoint her. 'Someone more or less perfect, then? You might have a bit of trouble finding him. We all have our faults.' His gaze now was a level one.

She only just stopped herself from saying, 'What? Even you?' She made do instead with, 'Well, I'll have to keep on looking then. Anyway, thanks for bringing me home. I could have walked — '

'Not on my watch,' he grimly said. 'Too many weirdos about these days. Anyway, thanks for coming. I'll see you around.' For a second his expression softened. 'Olivia needs someone like you in her life.' He paused. 'I've been wondering, would you like to meet up one evening for a drink, or maybe a meal?'

Wow! That was the very last question she'd expected. It took her a second or two to ask, 'Won't it be too late for Olivia?'

'You misunderstand me.' He smiled. 'I mean just you and me.'

Lauren was speechless. What the hell could she say? The mere idea of her and Nicholas spending a whole evening together, just the two of them, was enough to catapult her into a tailspin.

Yet really, what was she so afraid of? That she'd fall for him? That was a plausible worry, she conceded. She was already dangerously attracted to him. *Oh, stop it*, she told herself. Why was she so bothered? He was only asking her out for Olivia's sake — he'd more or less said that — not for the pleasure of her company, so it should be an easy enough matter to say no.

'Um, I'm a bit busy for the next week or two . . . '

Good grief, couldn't she have done better than that? He'd see straight through her words for the pathetic excuse that they were. She wasn't usually so inadequate with words. She'd always been able to hold her own in any conversation, more or less from the time she started to talk; at least that was what her mother always said.

She'd better go, she decided. It was the coward's way out, but what the hell? So, finishing what she'd begun only moments before, she swung the car door open and hurriedly climbed out. If it looked as if she was running away — well, she was.

'Okay.' Something flickered within his gaze then. Something that made her think he wasn't accustomed to being turned down and didn't much care for the experience. 'Maybe another time, then. See you.' With that, he revved the engine and within seconds was gone. She only just managed to close the door in time.

She stared after him, unsure quite what it was that had happened then. Had Nicholas Jordan actually asked her out on a date?

As incredible as that seemed, she rather thought he had.

3

Despite trying to put the whole thing from her mind, the question of who the man in the car could be continued to plague Lauren. However, it did look as if Nicholas was off the hook, because until he'd driven her home after their tea together he wouldn't have known her address. Although she supposed he could have looked her up in the telephone directory. One thing she did know, however: without doubt, the car wasn't his.

She made up her mind. It was most likely nothing more sinister than someone stopping to have a rest — although, she frowned, it did seem a strange place to choose to do that, on a fairly busy road, and to do it night after night.

It was just days after the tea party when she returned home from work to find the light flashing on her answer machine. She picked up a clearly hungry Sheba up before pressing the play button. The computerised voice informed her that she had just one message and the caller had withheld his number. She then heard a voice she didn't recognise: a man's voice — or at least she thought it was. It had a strange echoing quality, as if whoever was speaking was talking into something other than just the phone mouthpiece. That was enough to startle her, but what he went on to say despatched a chill right through her.

'I'm watching you. I'll always be watching you. Don't forget that.'

She hugged her cat close to her chest, as if Sheba could protect her in some way from the disembodied voice. For it could only mean one thing: someone had been out there, watching her.

But who could it be? Who would do such a thing? Someone who'd been at Fiona's party? It had all begun just days afterwards.

Her heartbeat rocketed as she tried

to recall who'd been there that evening, but it was a hopeless task. There'd been so many people there, a good half of them men. She wouldn't have noticed just one — possibly watching her even then?

She rang Fiona and asked who'd been there that evening; to see if someone, for any reason, stood out. She didn't say why she wanted to know.

'Good Lord,' Fiona cried, 'I haven't a clue. People turned up with friends and brought along friends of friends, some of them I didn't even know. Why?'

'Oh, no reason. I was trying to recall to tell Stella, as she wasn't able to be there.'

Which meant she was no nearer to identifying the culprit. Still, at the very least the phone call had confirmed that someone was indeed watching her. But whether that made things better or worse, she didn't know.

She sternly told herself it was just some crank, a nutter; someone a bit crazy, but ultimately harmless. She wasn't convinced by that argument, however. She went on to wonder whether, rather than it being one of the party guests, if it was someone who'd seen her in the street and had recognised her. Maybe even someone who was renting one of her houses? But they were all established couples. Why would one of them, completely out of the blue, decide to stalk her? It didn't seem plausible, and they were all newcomers to the village, in any case. No, it was more likely to be someone local; someone who knew her. She didn't know why she felt that way but she did. After all, he'd felt the need to disguise his voice, as if he were afraid she'd recognise him. And if he didn't already know them, it wouldn't be difficult to discover her address and phone number. She supposed it could even be one of her friends playing tricks on her.

It was then that she thought of Greg and recalled the tricks he and Paul had played at school. He had seemed offended when she'd refused to leave the party with him. But offended enough to do something like this? Something this scary? He'd been a mere boy in those days, full of high spirits and mischief; he was a grown man now and they were friends — weren't they? And something like this was beyond a mere trick.

* * *

Refusing to allow herself to be intimidated by what was happening, she carried on as normal: keeping herself busy, going to work, not allowing herself time to think about what was happening — which fortunately wasn't difficult, as business was booming. Henderson's Engineering specialised in designing and fitting custom-made equipment and machinery for the light engineering trade and their skills were very much in demand.

But then, as if things weren't already bad enough for Lauren, rumours began to circulate amongst the work force. The firm was one of a small group of three companies, a group which had been sold, so everyone was saying redundancies were to be expected.

'Who's bought it?' she asked Jonathon Rigsby, the man she was PA to.

'Jordan Enterprises.'

'Not Nicholas Jordan?' she gasped.

'Yeah, that's him.'

'But why? We've been making good profits recently.'

'That's why. Henderson wants to retire on a high, and who can blame him? He is getting on a bit now. Well past retirement age. Anyway, I've been offered another very lucrative position in Birmingham for loads more money; it's a much bigger business. There's more opportunity all round. There could even be a seat on the board of directors eventually. He shrugged. 'So I thought, why not? It's the perfect time to move on. I've been getting a bit bored here to be honest. In a bit of rut. I need a challenge. Anyway, as I've heard it, Jordan's looking to increase his portfolio by taking over smaller concerns and making them more efficient, resulting in even bigger profits. And from what I've heard, that usually means redundancies.' He shrugged again as if none of this was any of his concern — which, she supposed, it wasn't.

'So how many redundancies are we looking at?' she asked, wondering if this could be her cue to leave as well. She could devote herself then full-time to her buy-to-let business. She frowned. It was tempting, but could she really afford to lose her salary? The letting business brought in a good income, but would it be enough to live on and expand at the same time? The mortgage on her flat was quite high.

'Haven't a clue,' Jonathon said in answer to her question. 'You'll have to ask the man himself.'

Nicholas knew she worked at Henderson's. Not that that would make a scrap of difference to him. Still, she would have thought Henderson's Engineering too small to interest him. From what she'd heard, he usually went for larger, ailing companies — that way he minimised his costs, by buying at rock-bottom prices. Then, once he turned them around, he sold them on for a huge profit. He was obviously intending to accomplish something of that nature with Henderson's. The trouble was that to make larger profits in an already profitable business, as well as re-organising working methods for better efficiency, as Jonathon had said he'd have to get rid of a lot of the workforce as well. Drastically cut the overheads, in other words.

Which could well mean her losing her job and, after a rapid mental calculation, she didn't think she could afford to do that — not at present. Not if she wanted to go on investing in new properties. Her dream was to eventually own at least fifteen houses — in other words double her present portfolio. Twenty would be even better. She could then live comfortably on her profits. She would also fulfil her ambition to become a property tycoon of sorts.

* * *

But the likelihood or not of losing her job turned out to be the least of her worries.

Because the following evening, the phone rang at eight o'clock precisely and when she answered it, the same strangely disembodied voice whispered, 'Don't forget I'm watching you.'

She slammed the phone down without uttering a single word, before picking it up again and dialling 1471, whereupon she was told by the customary computerised tones that 'the caller's number has been withheld'.

* * *

And things weren't much better at work.

Henderson's had indeed been sold

and John Henderson had retired, to the south of France apparently. Jonathon also left just days after. Which left Lauren not having the faintest idea who she'd be working for on a daily basis. Come to that, she didn't even know whether she still had a job.

So she was split fairly evenly between relief and dismay when Nicholas Jordan strode into the office she'd shared with Jonathon and said, 'You'll be working as my PA now, Lauren, helping me to oversee this company as well as the other two.' He arched an eyebrow at her. 'You look surprised.'

'I was expecting to be made redundant.' And she was beginning to wish she had been. For how would she manage to avoid him now, as she'd firmly resolved to do? It would be impossible as his PA.

'Really? Why would you expect that? I need experienced people around me if I'm to achieve the results I want.'

'Well, don't you usually — uh, restructure the company and the workforce — which usually means high redundancy numbers?'

'Any redundancies I make are only ever voluntary.'

She was tempted to tell him that her friend Stella's hadn't been. From what she'd said at the time, she'd been more or less forced out. Or had that just been Stella's version of events? She had been known to wildly exaggerate on more than one occasion.

However, as his gaze had turned steely, she decided to opt for the easy route and say nothing. Not if she wanted to keep her job — for the time being at least.

'I'm not a hatchet man, Lauren, whatever you may have heard. I always try to work with people, not against them. I'm very much a hands-on person so I'll be around on a daily basis — for a while, at least. We'll split our time between here and the other two companies.'

'I see.' Once again, what he was saying was the complete opposite to what Stella had told her. There he hadn't shown his face, never mind his hands. So why was he intending to be so involved at Henderson's? The thought crept in and wouldn't be dismissed — could it be because of her?

'Is that all acceptable?'

Lauren simply nodded. For the moment, and quite uncharacteristically, words were beyond her.

'So if you'll grab your notepad, we'll discuss the day's — no, make that the week's work.' His tone was such that he might have been talking to a complete stranger.

All Lauren could think was, maybe she should take the coward's way out after all and hand in her notice right now. The mere idea of working for this granite-faced man — so different to Jonathon's easy-going manner — was a daunting one. All signs of any previous amicability had vanished. He was now all businessman: hard-eyed, determined, uncompromising.

Something in her expression must

have revealed her doubts, because he looked directly at her and said, 'Lauren, we'll get along fine.'

Easy for him to say. She had a very strong suspicion that Nicholas Jordan was going to turn out to be a difficult and demanding boss. He wouldn't have reached the dizzy heights he had in the world of finance, and so made the fortune he was now in possession of, if he wasn't. She sighed softly. Everything was about to change, that was more than evident — the last thing she needed, considering what was happening in her private life.

* * *

With the efficiency she'd expected, Nicholas outlined the whole of the following week's work. He clearly didn't believe in wasting time, his or that of the people he was paying, and she couldn't fault him for that. But the list, when Lauren had time to study it in more detail, told her she was going to be expected to earn every pound of the wage he'd be paying her. Not that she minded that, and there was nothing on her pad she wasn't capable of doing.

She set to work and very soon had forgotten all about her stalker. And when she did briefly think of him, she quickly told herself it couldn't possibly be Nicholas. Whatever else he might be — slave driver, martinet — he didn't strike her as the type to intentionally frighten a woman. That person had to be some sort of lone oddball; one who, in the event of no sort of response from her, would, she was sure, swiftly tire of his crazy game-playing.

Which only made it all the more depressing to receive the text message on her mobile phone that evening. A totally different sort of message to last time, making her wonder whether it could be two different people behind it all. But that was highly unlikely, surely? Two people — what? Stalking her? Harassing her? Persecuting her, even? Because that was what it was beginning to feel like. Persecution.

It said, 'You'll be getting some flowers tomorrow to show you how much I love you. Hope you like them — I know you like lilies. Bye, my lamb. I'll call later.'

Who on earth — ?

Whoever it was had blocked his number once again. She hadn't even realised you could do that on a mobile phone. It couldn't be Nicholas. She could imagine him sending flowers, but not to her, and certainly he wouldn't call her his 'lamb'. Their relationship now was one of professionalism only. And anyway, how had whoever-it-was got her mobile number? She didn't just give that out to anyone.

Oh no. In a single, illuminating flash she remembered she'd given it on her answer machine. She'd been expecting a call from an electrician, and not wanting to miss it, she'd left him a message asking him to call her on her mobile. She'd needed another electrical socket in her bedroom for a second lamp. Hadn't she erased the number afterwards? She checked and, sure enough, she hadn't. The anonymous caller must have called her house phone again at some time when she wasn't at home and, taking advantage of that, made a note of her mobile number.

But it was the changed tone of the message that particularly worried her. Instead of the threatening words 'I'll be watching you', it was now the indisputable words of a lover.

What was he playing at?

She rushed to the window that overlooked the street, half expecting to see the familiar vehicle below, but there was no sign of it.

* * *

As if all that wasn't enough, she arrived at work the following morning to find Nicholas waiting in the office, already working, and with another lengthy list of tasks for her.

The man was a workaholic and clearly expected her to be the same. This list would take hours — no, days — to complete. As a result, they worked right through, not even breaking for lunch. She was so hungry by five o'clock she would have eaten anything that was offered to her, even a cardboard box. Her stomach rumbled loudly, so loudly that Nicholas heard it and grinned.

'Come on, I'll treat you to something to eat. I think we both deserve it, and as you turned me down the other evening . . . '

'Oh no, really, I couldn't.'

'No arguments, I insist. It will demonstrate that I'm not a complete slave-driver.'

'Don't you have to get home to Olivia?' Desperate, she cast around for an excuse; any excuse.

'Not tonight. She's gone to a birthday party and she's having a — sleepover. Is that what they call it?'

'I believe so.'

'So — ?' He regarded her expectantly.

All of a sudden he looked so much like his daughter, his expression one of unmistakable pleading, that she didn't have it in her to refuse.

'In that case, thank you. That would be . . . nice.'

Amusement glittered at her. 'I'd hoped for something a bit more enthusiastic than 'nice'.' He deliberately emphasized the final word.

'Okay.' She couldn't help but grin at him. 'Great. Is that better?'

'Definitely. I've booked a table at the Bistro in Kingsford.'

'You've booked — ?' Had he been so confident that she'd agree to eat with him? Irritation flared within her. Such arrogant self-assurance. She should have expected it, she supposed. It wasn't the first time he'd revealed that side of himself, after all. She was sorely tempted then to turn him down, say she'd changed her mind.

'Just in case you said yes.' His

expression told her he'd sensed her vexation at his presumption. Could the wretched man, as well as possessing numerous other talents — not least the ability to make tons of money — also be a mind-reader? If he was, it would make life very difficult now that she was working with him, not to say downright uncomfortable. 'It's a very popular place, with a waiting list usually. I got lucky. Um, do you want to go home and freshen up? Maybe change?'

Oh Lord, was she whiffy after her hectic day? Surreptitiously, she lowered her head and sniffed. No. So was she not dressed appropriately? Was it a very smart restaurant? She didn't have a clue, never having been there previously. She couldn't have afforded it if what she'd heard about its prices was true, and the men she'd gone out with certainly couldn't have.

'Um . . . ' She glanced down over her cashmere top and tight, just-above-the-knee skirt.

'You look fine to me,' Nicholas gently assured her.

So he could read minds. Heavens above, was she to have no privacy at all? Not even inside her own head? Well, he wasn't going have things all his own way.

So, just to be contrary, she said, 'Do you know, I will pop home. I could use a shower.' Her flat was only a couple of minutes' drive away, in any case. She had plenty of time — or she presumed she did. 'What time's the table booked for?'

'Seven o'clock. There's no rush. I'm sure they'll keep the table for me, even if we're a bit late.'

Yes, she mused, she was sure they would. They wouldn't want to get on the wrong side of such a wealthy client, after all.

'I'll pick you up at six thirty.'

4

Lauren had to park her car several yards away from the entrance to her flat, it being the only roadside space available. Not that there was anything unusual about that. It wasn't until she climbed from the driver's seat and turned to pull her handbag out that she noticed Sam standing in the doorway of the butcher's shop opposite, watching her. He was holding a broom, so presumably he'd been sweeping up before closing for the day.

In a bid to be friendly, she raised a hand in greeting and smiled, to no avail. He immediately looked away and applied himself once more to his cleaning.

What a strange man he was, she mused. One minute watching her with interest, the next ignoring her. He was extremely shy — she'd realised that from her dealings with him in the shop — to the point of seeming shifty, and she'd always been suspicious of anyone who wouldn't meet her gaze, invariably asking herself what it was they were trying to hide.

She turned away and headed for her flat. She couldn't believe she'd let Nicholas talk her into having dinner with him. The tea party had been bad enough, but that was nothing compared to an entire evening with just the two of them. Her heart sank at the prospect. Could she phone him and cancel? Or would that be discourteous? Yes, she grudgingly admitted, it would be.

She was halfway up the stairs when her phone beeped, signalling an incoming text message. Maybe it was Nicholas; maybe he, too, had had second thoughts? She stopped, pulled her phone from her pocket, and looked at the screen. Again, there was no name displayed, other than 'blocked call'. It couldn't be Nicholas; she belatedly realised he didn't have her mobile number. It must be her stalker. For heaven's sake, why didn't he leave her alone? She jabbed at the button and read it.

'Hi, have you had my flowers? What do you think? Are they beautiful? Nothing's too good for the woman I adore. Talk to you soon.'

She leapt up the rest of the stairs, taking them two at a time, and there they were, propped up against her front door: an enormous cellophane-wrapped bouquet of white lilies. Their perfume filled the landing, sickly sweet and suffocating. Lauren hated lilies and if her caller had really been her lover, he'd have known that.

She picked them up, unlocked her front door, strode into the kitchen and rammed them into the pedal bin. She then deleted both text messages, the first one and this one, before realising how stupid that was. They were evidence, the only evidence she possessed so far of what was happening to her. She'd even deleted the answer phone message. What a moron!

All of a sudden she was glad she was going out, even if it was with Nicholas Jordan. If she hadn't been, she'd have spent the evening going over and over all that was happening, trying to work out who it could be and what she should do about it. Maybe she should simply go to the police; let them deal with it. But with no evidence to show them, would they believe her? Or would they put it all down to the ravings of a hysterical woman?

She fed Sheba, saying, 'Sorry, sweetie, I'm afraid I'm off out again. I'll stay in tomorrow, I promise.' Guilt suffused her. She'd found herself a cat for company, and now she hardly seemed to be here.

Sheba regarded her, her expression blank. She didn't even meow, not the teeniest sound. Now Lauren really did feel bad.

After a quick shower, she opened her wardrobe door and pulled out the first thing that she saw. It just happened to be her favourite dress: forget-me-not blue, V-necked, not too low. She hadn't forgotten Nicholas's searching gaze at the party and the way it had made her feel — practically naked. It had three-quarter sleeves and a short fitted skirt. She teamed it with deeper blue, slender heeled shoes and a matching fitted jacket. A blue-and-pink scarf draped around her neck completed her outfit just in time.

A car horn sounded from the street below, imperious and demanding. She pulled a face at her pet and muttered, 'The boss is summoning me.'

Sheba, still sulking, gave no response. Instead, in an unmistakable show of rebellion, she curled up on the quilt — something she wasn't normally allowed to do in Lauren's absence — thereby readying herself for an after-dinner sleep.

Lauren grabbed a handbag, making sure she had her key, and left the flat, double-checking that the door was closed and securely locked before running down the stairs.

Nicholas made no comment on her appearance other than for a brief glance over her and a fleeting smile. She had no idea whether he approved of how she looked or not. Which was vexing, considering that she'd made the effort to return home and change out of her workday clothes.

'Are you okay?' he finally asked.

'Yes.' For a split second she was tempted to tell him what was happening to her, but common sense won out and she stayed silent. After all, she couldn't be sure — one-hundred-percent sure — that her stalker wasn't him; and if it was, she didn't want to give him the satisfaction of knowing she was bothered about it.

* * *

The Bistro, when they arrived, was already three-quarters full of extremely elegant people, just as Lauren had anticipated. She shrugged off her jacket and hung it over the back of her chair, then watched as Nicholas's heavy-lidded eyes skimmed over her, lingering momentarily upon her exposed throat and chest, mutely but very visibly appreciating the couple of inches of cleavage that her neckline revealed. Her pulse upped its rate into racing speed — much to her annoyance. She refused to acknowledge her growing feelings of attraction to him, other than to resolve to rid herself of them and quickly.

They'd no sooner taken their seats than the maître d' arrived, so after a quick scan of the menu they both ordered. Nicholas opted for the smoked trout and then a rare steak; Lauren plumped for the Greek salad to be followed by a rack of lamb with baby potatoes and a selection of fresh vegetables.

'And we'll have a bottle of Moet, please,' Nicholas went on to order, 'which we'll have straight away.' He grinned at Lauren. 'I think we deserve it after the hard slog of today. Thank you, by the way, for the enormous amount of work which you've got through. You've gone way beyond the call of duty.'

'It was nothing,' she modestly replied. 'I aim to please.'

'Oh, believe me, you do that all right,' Nicholas throatily murmured.

As Lauren was wondering precisely what that remark signified, the wine waiter brought the champagne, popped the cork somewhat flamboyantly, and poured them each a glassful.

Nicholas lifted his at once in a salute to Lauren. 'Here's to a successful partnership.'

Partnership? Lauren thought. What did he mean? She wasn't his partner; far from it. Trying not to be too obvious about it, she carefully considered him, but his expression revealed nothing of his thoughts. He was clearly a master of dissimulation. And that might prove tricky, working with him as closely as she would be. She'd been able to read Jonathon as easily as she would the open pages of a book, and so could take whatever steps were necessary to keep him happy. That clearly wouldn't be happening with Nicholas.

The food when it arrived was delicious, and once again Lauren cleared every morsel from her plate. Nicholas made no secret of his bemusement as she scooped up the last remnants of her lamb and vegetables, and yet again she wondered, slightly uncomfortably, if he thought her a pig.

'Dessert?' he asked, the corners of his mouth quirking with what she suspected was amusement.

'Yes, please.' She returned his gaze defiantly. He waved the waiter over. 'Dessert menu, please.'

She took one glance at the menu and without hesitation ordered, 'Crème brulee, please.' It was her absolute favourite. Nicholas declined anything.

'I'm amazed you stay so slim,' he commented as she scraped her plate clean and leant back in her seat with an unashamedly contented sigh.

'Nervous energy,' she countered. 'It burns up all the calories.'

'You don't strike me as being the nervous type.'

Huh! What did he know? He was making her nervous for one thing, and the anonymous stalker certainly had her on edge.

'So tell me,' he said, 'what do you do with yourself when you're not working?'

'Oh, meet friends, watch TV, read . . . I do some of the work on my buy-to-let properties — not as much as I did in the beginning. They usually need some sort of renovation to make them rentable.'

'How do you find the time for that, with your work as a PA?'

'I do it in the evenings mostly. It's mainly decorating. The more complicated stuff I leave to the experts.'

'Such as?'

'Fitting new kitchens, bathrooms, that sort of thing. I have had a go at putting flat-pack furniture together.

'You amaze me.' And he did look

gratifyingly astonished. 'Maybe you could help me out at the house. You're clearly a woman of considerable talent.'

'Oh no, I don't think so,' she smoothly responded. 'That would be well out of my comfort zone.'

'That's a shame,' he murmured. 'It would be good to work together — hands-on.' His look now was one of sheer provocation.

'I thought we already did that,' she once again smoothly riposted.

He gave a deep chuckle. 'That wasn't quite what I meant.'

Desperate to change the subject away from herself, she jumped in to ask, 'What do you do for pleasure when you're not working?'

'Not a lot. I'm afraid I tend to take my work home with me, and then, of course, there's Olivia. I like to spend as much time as I can with her. And I do like going to the theatre. How about you?'

She had her mouth open to say she didn't really have the time, when a sultry voice drawled from behind her, 'Nicholas, darling, I called at the house and Mrs Hodges told me you were here, so I thought I'd join you.'

Lauren swivelled her head and found herself looking directly up into the flawlessly lovely face of Serena, Nicholas's ex-wife.

'Won't you introduce me?' she purred softly, although the hardness within her eyes gave the lie to the show of friendliness. Serena wasn't at all pleased to see Lauren with Nicholas, clearly enjoying an intimate meal for two. 'Celebrating?' she went on, her gaze moving to the bottle of champagne.

Lauren swept her gaze back to Nicholas. His features were glacial as he regarded his wife, just as his eyes were.

'Hello, Serena. Yes, we are celebrating what I'm sure will be a very successful partnership by the look of things. You must remember Lauren from our school days. Weren't you in the same year?'

'Were we?' Serena drawled. 'I really don't recall — Lauren?' She cast her gaze upwards as if puzzling over Lauren's identity.

'You'd have known me as Ann,' Lauren interjected. 'I changed it to Lauren once I left school.'

'Oh yes, I do remember you. You always had your head in a book. A real swot. Tell me, what did you do for fun?'

'Oh, lots.' Lauren deliberately left it vague. She had no intention of confessing that her evenings, as well as her days, had usually been spent studying, so determined was she to do well.

Serena smiled condescendingly, leading Lauren to recall how she'd always preferred boys to books, which meant she'd eventually left school with nothing much in the way of qualifications — other than the skills needed to ensnare a rich husband. But she was being catty now, Lauren chided herself.

Serena turned back to Nicholas. 'I've only come for a flying visit. I thought I could stay at the Grange, spend time with Olivia.'

Nicholas's one eyebrow zoomed upwards. 'At a loose end, are we?' he sarcastically asked. 'Where's Rupert?'

'Away on business. Darling, I really don't wish to discuss my private affairs in front of a stranger.'

'Lauren's not a stranger.'

'She is to me. Look — my luggage is still in the car; I didn't bother going in to unpack. Maybe I could join you and then we could return to the house together, just you and I, Nicholas.'

'I don't think so,' Nicholas bluntly retorted. 'Lauren and I are discussing business. She's my PA, so there's lots to talk about.'

Lauren thought it was time she made things a bit clearer. 'Actually, I think we're finished, Nicholas, so if you want to return home with Serena . . . '

Nicholas held her gaze with his own. He looked as if he were about to say something, but then changed his mind and waited for her to go on.

' . . . I can get a taxi home,' she finished.

'You most certainly will not,' he said. 'I brought you, and I'll take you home again. Here.' he pulled a bunch of keys from his pocket and handed them to Serena. 'Let yourself in. Mrs Hodges will have retired to her own suite for the night. You can have the blue bedroom. Left at the top of the stairs. First door on your right. Oh — and Olivia's not at home; she's having a sleepover.'

Serena pouted. 'Yes, Mrs Hodges told me. It's very disappointing. I'm sure she'll be thrilled to see her mummy. Maybe I could ring her — although it might be a little late, I suppose.'

'Oh, do you think she'll remember who you are?' was Nicholas's terse response to that.

'Now, now, darling. I'm sure — um, Laura, wasn't it?'

'Lauren, actually,' Lauren murmured. Serena had looked charmingly uncertain but Lauren knew she'd remembered her name perfectly well; she just wanted to pretend she hadn't. It was an intentional slight.

'Lauren doesn't want to listen to our tedious family business.'

'I'm sure she doesn't, so if you'd like to return to the Grange, leave the front door on the latch and I'll see you in the morning.' He paused then. 'Or maybe not. I'll be leaving the house before eight and I know you can't do without your lie-ins.' His tone then was one of pure sarcasm.

Serena pouted once more, not so charmingly this time. She was clearly irritated by Nicholas's offhand manner towards her, as well as his unmistakable dismissal of her. She did, however, take the not-so-subtle hint and wished them both a cool goodbye and left.

Lauren wished herself anywhere but where she was. She began to get to her feet. Nicholas frowned at her. 'Where are you going?'

'I don't want to get in the way, and I'm sure you want to — '

'Sit down.'

Now it was her turn to regard him resentfully. Who did he think he was, ordering her about? Mind you, she should have expected it, she supposed. That natural arrogance was bound to eventually break free. He'd managed to keep it under a tight rein so far, but —

'I was about to order coffee.' He signalled to the waiter. 'Two coffees, please.'

Lauren didn't say a word. She certainly wasn't about to tell him she didn't drink coffee in the evening. He and Serena made a good pair, both overconfident that what they wanted was paramount. Of course, that wouldn't make for a good relationship — hence their divorce, presumably. In fact, it was a wonder the marriage had lasted long enough to produce Olivia, if this evening had been an example of how they'd behaved when together. Yet they must have loved each other once.

Nicholas glanced back at Lauren. 'Don't take any notice of anything

Serena said. So tell me, what do you do for relaxation these days? There's apparently no man in your life.'

'Who says?'

His gaze narrowed. 'I thought you did.'

'Well, you thought wrong. Just because I'm not wearing a ring, it doesn't mean I don't see anyone. I do, on a casual basis,' she lied. Suddenly it seemed important that he didn't know that the last date she'd been on was a full six months ago and that it had been an unmitigated disaster. Mark Sinclair had been his name. A friend had introduced them at a party, and she'd agreed to meet him for a drink the following evening. However, when his conversation had been a non-stop monologue about himself and his dog, she'd eventually made her excuses and left.

'Greg Mallory?'

'Why would you think that?' she carefully asked.

He shrugged. 'You seemed close at

Fiona's party. Although — ' His eyes gleamed at her. ' — I noticed you didn't leave together. How come?'

'He wanted to go, I didn't.'

He didn't say anything; just considered her, his expression a reflective one.

She decided to turn the tables. 'Are you seeing anyone?' Disconcertingly, she realised she really rather wanted to know.

'Not at present. Between Olivia and work, I'm kept pretty busy. Although I can make myself available — to the right person,' he then added with a wry grin.

The waiter placed their coffees in front of them, cutting short their conversation and leaving Lauren wondering what exactly he'd meant by that last remark.

Suddenly, wanting nothing more than for this evening to be over, Lauren lifted her cup and drank the liquid straight down, even though it was really too hot — burning her throat as she did so.

Nicholas regarded her with astonishment. She smiled nonchalantly back.

'If you're ready to go, I certainly am,' she said. 'And I'm sure Serena will be at home impatiently awaiting you.' A shaft of pure jealousy stabbed her then, at the image she'd conjured up of the two of them together — alone.

For God's sake, she irritably demanded of herself, what the hell did it matter what they did? It was no concern of hers, and she didn't want it to be. Yet somehow, that thought didn't have the ring of authenticity that she'd hoped for.

* * *

Nicholas drove her back to her flat, conversation between them non-existent. He parked on the road outside and courteously walked around to open her door. She climbed out and well — she didn't know what happened, but her heel slipped off the kerb edge and she felt herself start to fall.

Nicholas lunged and caught her, holding her upright before sliding his arms around her, pulling her close and so clamping their bodies together. The sheer power of him rendered her breathless.

'Sorry.'

'Don't be,' was his throaty reply. He bent his head as he spoke to drop a kiss upon her parted lips. Before she could even begin to respond, he pulled away again.

She stared at him, at his eyes, mere slits now as they glittered back at her. His mouth, when her gaze fell to it, remained dangerously close. She sighed and closed her eyes, expecting — no, wanting a second kiss suddenly quite desperately.

When nothing happened, she stared up at him, puzzled. Hadn't he enjoyed their kiss? Had she disappointed him in some way?

He was watching her closely as she turned all this over in her head, but all he said was, 'Good night, Lauren. I'll see you tomorrow.'

Yet something in his expression told her that again, he'd had no trouble reading her thoughts; in particular, her disappointment at his restraint.

And how embarrassing was that?

5

She watched Nicholas drive away, still unsure what to make of what had just happened between them. It was as she turned towards the door that led up to her flat that she noticed a light in the window above Jameson's, the butcher's. A man was standing there with the curtains drawn back; he was looking directly down at her.

Why — it was Sam. He must live above the shop. She hadn't realised that. She waved a greeting, just as she had earlier; and just as had happened then, he turned away.

What was his problem? She was only trying to be friendly; he was a neighbour, after all. Maybe, she belatedly wondered, he didn't care for women? Maybe men were more his thing? He certainly appeared frightened of women — or was it just her that scared him?

Not surprisingly, the events of the evening — especially that unexpected kiss — didn't help her to sleep. Not even the warmth of Sheba curled up against her feet on top of the duvet induced her to relax, and by the time the clock displayed 1:00 on its screen, she gave up the attempt and got up, intending to make herself a cup of hot chocolate. That usually helped if she really couldn't sleep — which, truth to tell, wasn't that often. It might even banish the memories of Nicholas and his kiss, as fleeting as it had been.

Because, let's face it, he could have prolonged things, extended the brushing of lips into something more passionate, but he'd chosen not to, so that told her all she needed to know. It had merely been a way of ending the evening, a perfunctory gesture on his part. She mustn't read anything more into it than it being Nicholas's way of thanking her for the hard work she'd put in that day — or maybe for an enjoyable evening. Enjoyable, that was, until Serena turned up and set about spoiling it.

And that, Lauren guessed, had been quite intentional. She hadn't liked seeing Nicholas with another woman, even though they were divorced.

She sipped at her chocolate and walked across to the window that looked down onto the street. Just as she got there, her mobile phone, which was on the coffee table in front of the settee, beeped. She went and picked it up and saw that she had an incoming text message. With a sinking feeling, she pressed the button to read it and as before the words 'blocked caller' appeared, followed by the text.

'Look out of the window,' it directed.

She hurriedly did. At first, she thought there was no-one out there. She certainly couldn't see the car that had been there before. She gazed up and down the street, and then she saw what looked like a man's figure standing in the dark on the opposite side of the road, completely motionless. He was holding something in his hand. Her phone beeped once again, another message. This time it said, 'I'm watching you. I'm always watching you.'

Lauren gasped and read it again more slowly before returning her gaze to the street below, to the spot where she'd seen him standing. But he'd disappeared — in the moment or two it had taken her to read and reread his message, he'd gone.

How had he managed to move that quickly, and who the hell was he? How long had he been standing out there? If it was someone who supposedly cared for her, why was he doing something like this?

And what was he playing at? He started off by sending threatening messages, then decided to change them to what amounted to love notes, and then it was back to threats once more. It was crazy. Could he be crazy, as she'd wondered once before? Someone who should be in care, but wasn't?

In which case, he could be dangerous.

She'd read about people like this; seriously disturbed people. They became fixated on someone and interpreted the merest glance, casual smile, anything really, as a loving gesture meant solely for them. They imagined a real relationship existed when in actual fact the object of their passion didn't know they even existed. But, Lauren frowned, the victim was usually a celebrity, someone famous. Not a complete unknown like her.

And looked at rationally, he must know her, because he knew where she lived. And he knew her phone number. But then if he knew her name and address, he could look up her number in the phone directory. Or maybe he'd already known it? Which again must mean she knew him.

She left the window and returned to the settee. Sheba sprang up beside her and lay, stretching her length along the side of her thigh. Absent-mindedly, Lauren stroked her. The cat began to purr, wriggling and stretching her body even further in an ecstasy of pleasure.

'What shall I do, Sheba?' She then gave a snort of laughter. Maybe it was her who was losing her mind: for heaven's sake, asking an animal — even an animal as responsive and intelligent as Sheba was — what she should do. Did she expect the cat to tell her?

* * *

The following morning, after very little sleep, she was exhausted, depressed, and with a headache the like of which she'd never before experienced — not even in the aftermath of overdoing things in the alcohol department. In fact, it was so severe she'd barely been able to lift her head from the pillow without groaning out loud in pain. Not even Sheba's plaintive meowing for her breakfast could initially inspire her to move. Eventually of course she did, but it had taken three cups of tea and two paracetamol tablets before she began to feel anything like human. A hot shower had completed her recovery — or so she thought. She soon discovered how wrong she was. Because when she arrived at work, Nicholas took one look at her and unceremoniously asked, 'Are you okay?'

She nodded, only to immediately wish she hadn't. For the jarring pain that subsequently pounded within her head made her feel nauseous enough to consider a dash to the loo.

'You don't look it, if I may say so.'

'Too much champagne, maybe?' she murmured, even though she knew it wasn't that. As she recalled, she'd barely drunk two glassfuls.

Nicholas cocked his head to one side as he proceeded to confirm her own recollection of things. 'I don't recall you drinking that much of it. In fact, we ended up leaving some in the bottle. Are you sure that's all that's wrong? You look — '

'What?' she snapped. Did he have to go on and on about it? Did the man have no tact? Telling a woman she didn't look well was not the most effective way of charming her. Mind you, he probably wasn't interested in charming her. She was a mere employee, after all. She shouldn't read too much into his invitation to dinner. He'd made it perfectly clear that it was his way of thanking her for her hard work — end of story.

So, why did that reflection so depress her?

'Troubled would be the best description of how you look.'

'Well, maybe the strain of working for a new boss is getting to me,' she curtly said.

'What, even a new boss who took you to dinner?' His expression was a wry one. 'I'd hardly have thought that was a particularly stressful way of spending an evening.'

She shrugged. 'Yes, thank you for that. I don't believe I said it last night.'

'Well, we were otherwise occupied as I recall,' he murmured provocatively. He must be referring to their kiss.

'How's Serena?' she hurriedly asked, desperate to change the subject. 'I hope she found her way back to Markham Grange okay?'

'She did.'

His gaze, she belatedly realised, hadn't left her since she'd first arrived. 'I haven't seen her since. Serena doesn't realise a time exists before eleven o'clock.'

'Have you seen Olivia?' She was beginning to feel uncomfortable beneath those darkly brooding eyes. Mainly because there was an air of simmering tension growing between them; a tension that was intensifying by the second.

'No. Fern will collect her.'

'Oh, good; that's good. I'm sure she'll be pleased to see her mother; she must miss her. I know I would have at her age.' *Stop gabbling*, she told herself. It was a dead giveaway that she was nervous.

But Nicholas didn't seem to notice, because he went on to say, 'I want to put together some sort of plan for a more efficient method of processing orders. I'd be glad of your input.'

And that was that. He'd instantly reverted to the professional business-man once more. How did he do that? It was the sort of behaviour a chameleon would exhibit, temper and mood changing from one second to another. It was a wonder he didn't change colour too.

She then found herself asking — could Nicholas, with the same effortless ease, transform himself from a charming, sexy escort to a threatening and possibly delusional stalker?

Once again, she worked practically non-stop all day. So much so, that she was heartily relieved when five o'clock came and she could leave. If it was going to continue like this, she might well end up pleading to be made redundant. She'd take the money, however much it might be, and run.

As the morning had been a dry one, she'd decided to walk to work — it only took ten minutes — in the hope that the autumnal chill might rid her of the after-effects of her disturbed night. Needless to say, it hadn't. As she walked from the office now, she bitterly regretted that decision, because she was greeted with torrential rain. Practically a monsoon, in fact. And she hadn't even brought an umbrella with her. Exasperated, she peered out from the doorway. She would be well and truly soaked through by the time she reached home.

Whatever had she been thinking of? Her jacket, as warm as it had been this morning, would offer little in the way of protection from such a deluge. However, she excused herself by reasoning that her lack of forethought was perfectly understandable given the way she'd felt first thing. Oh well, there was nothing for it but to brave the elements. So she'd get wet. It wasn't the end of the world.

'Hey, Lauren, want a lift?'

She breathed a sigh of relief. It was Greg, and he was in a very expensive-looking sporty BMW. Crikey, he'd done well for himself. 'You're a sight for sore eyes,' she now called. 'I'd be extremely glad of a lift.'

She darted across the pavement, taking care to avoid the series of puddles, and practically flung herself through the door that Greg was holding open for her. She didn't notice Nicholas coming out of the factory behind her, just as she didn't see the expression that darkened his eyes at the sight of her going off with Greg.

'Whew!' she cried, smoothing down her wet hair with her fingertips and shaking the raindrops from her jacket. 'So much for my decision to walk this morning. I won't be doing that again in a hurry,' she laughed across at him. 'This is a nice car,' she went on to remark, glancing approvingly at the fancy dashboard and the luxurious leather seats.

'A present to myself for my last birthday. All I have to do now, of course, is pay for it.' He too laughed, seemingly not at all concerned about the prospect of that. He also seemed to have forgotten his vexation with her at Fiona's party, when she'd turned down his invitation to leave and go for a drink instead. 'So,' he went on with a slanting glance at Lauren, at the same time accelerating sufficiently to make his tyres slip on the streams of water running along the surface of the road, 'how're you doing? With the new boss?'

'You've heard then?'

He nodded. 'Everybody's heard. You know what this village is like.'

'It's fine,' she replied. 'A bit hectic at the moment. He's kept me on as his PA. I was half-expecting to be made redundant.'

'That's good.'

'Yes, I just hope I'm up to the job. It's more stressful than previously. He likes things done his way, which maybe isn't such a bad thing. It had all got a bit sloppy.'

He gave a snort of what sounded like sardonic mirth. 'I'm sure Jordan will soon have that all pulled into shape, along with the employees.' He slanted another glance at her. 'So he's forgiven you for your criticisms of his renovation work at Markham Grange then?'

'Apparently so,' she said, looking away from Greg's searching gaze.

'And is everything I've heard about him correct?'

She turned her head to look at him again. 'Depends what you've heard.'

'Oh, just that he'll do whatever it takes to get what he wants. The last place he bought, he sacked half of the workforce, brought in new work practices and then sold it again for twice what he paid for it. Be warned, Lauren, he's the archetypical hatchet-man.'

Lauren couldn't help wondering then just what Nicholas would resort to to get what he wanted. Kiss his employee, to encourage her to work even harder?

No, she was being unfair now. He had a perfect right to expect the best she could give to her job. She was well paid. And if that meant the occasional spot of overtime, then so be it. Still, there was no denying that he had grabbed the opportunity of her losing her balance to kiss her. She frowned.

'You okay?' Greg asked, his expression one of concern now. 'I haven't worried you with my remarks, have I? Look, if he sacks you, there's a job at my firm. We're always on the lookout for trustworthy people, especially ones with a good brain as well. Which clearly you have. We could train you; it wouldn't take that long. Give me a bell if you're interested.' Greg worked for a company who designed tailor-made computer systems for other companies. 'Because, let's face it, that's the future. Computers are replacing people more and more. I can envisage the day when just a couple of operators will run a huge factory. The work will all be done by computer-controlled robots.'

'I'll remember that, Greg.'

A job with Greg would be something to fall back on, she supposed. Although how well she'd do in his high-tech world of computer programme designing, she wasn't sure.

'Good. Here we are then. This is where you live, isn't it?'

'Yeah.'

'I've seen you coming out a couple of times so I guessed it was. Look, give me your business card if you have one.'

'Um — hang on.' She groped inside her handbag. Oh, damn. She hadn't got one on her. How had that happened? She always carried some. 'Sorry, I'll have to let you have one some other time.'

'Okay.' He groped inside his jacket pocket and brought out a small notepad. 'Just for now, give me your numbers, mobile and house phone.'

She did.

'And email address — just in case. I can keep you up to date on any vacancies that we have.'

She readily gave it all to him, only to almost at once think maybe she shouldn't be so ready to tell people these things. Not in the light of what was happening to her. Yet, how could she conduct her business if she didn't?

Oh, for goodness sake, she'd known Greg since school. No matter what she'd previously thought, her stalker was highly unlikely to be him, practical joker or not.

'Here's my card, so you can get in touch if you need to.'

She glanced at it. His email address, mobile and house phone numbers, even his home address — it was all there. No 1, Rose Cottages, High Street.

'I've only lived there for six months,' he told her. 'They've been renovated. I'm surprised you weren't interested in them, although I have bought mine, not rented.'

It must be one of the terrace of three small houses on the periphery of the village, the opposite end to where she had her flat and where the factory was.

Which meant she'd only ever had reason to drive past them once or twice, and that would have been before Greg moved there.

'I've just had a thought. Do you fancy going out tonight?' His smile lit up his face, making his eyes sparkle. He was making no attempt to hide his admiration of her. 'We could do our catching up.'

'I'd love that.' And she would. It would also serve as a distraction from the worries about her stalker. She suppressed the rising of guilt at the notion of poor Sheba being left alone again. She was an animal who liked human company, especially Lauren's.

'Good. We'll go to the Bistro in Kingsford.' She didn't really know why, but she didn't tell him that Nicholas had taken her to the same place the evening before. 'I'll book a table when I get home.'

As she'd been planning a solitary evening in, she'd taken up Tom Jameson's suggestion that she email her meat order to pick up on her way home. It had hardly seemed worthwhile for two lamb chops, so she'd also included a steak and a couple of pork chops for her freezer. She'd just about be in time to pick it all up before the shop closed.

Mind you, if Greg couldn't manage to reserve a table she might still end up eating a chop on her own.

6

Greg succeeded in getting a table at the Bistro; they'd had a cancellation, he told her. She still didn't mention Nicholas taking her the evening before, which was a mistake because the warmth of the head waiter's smile made it obvious he remembered her. Diplomatically though, and in the manner of any good maître d', he made no mention of it. Nonetheless, she saw Greg taking note of the smile. However, it wasn't until they were seated at their table that he said, 'The maître d' looks as if he knows you. Have you been here before?'

'Yes, last night.'

He regarded her with surprise, but waited until they'd ordered their drinks from the hovering waiter before asking, 'Last night? Why didn't you say? We could have gone somewhere else. Who did you come with?'

'Nicholas.'

'Jordan! My God, he didn't waste any time in wining and dining you.'

'It was his way of thanking me for all the work I'd done.' Although why she was making excuses she didn't know. It was none of Greg's business what she did and with whom.

'So you don't mind coming here again tonight?'

'No, not at all. I loved the food, and the champagne was — '

'Champagne?' he burst out, as if he could contain his irritation no longer. He'd spoken loudly enough to attract the attention of some nearby diners.

Now it was Lauren's turn to be irritated. Once again, it was nothing to do with Greg whether they'd had champagne or not, and she hated being the focus of other people's attention like this.

'Are you sure he wasn't after something else? Because I feel I should warn you — ' Greg's eyes were glittering now, and it wasn't with admiration. ' — he made a pest of himself a while ago. He and his PA went away for a couple of days to sort out some business with a customer, and he wasted no time in propositioning her.'

'Propositioning her?' What century was Greg living in? Early nineteenth? She burst out laughing. 'You make him sound like some sort of Casanova.'

His mouth tightened as his face flamed. 'It wasn't funny, I can assure you,' he snapped. 'He forced his way into her room.'

Lauren stopped laughing at that point. 'What? No, he wouldn't.'

'Oh, he did. Not so funny now, is it? What I'm saying is, just watch yourself, Lauren. Some men in his position — well, they expect to enjoy a variety of extra benefits with their PA.'

'Who told you this?' she demanded. 'The woman herself?'

'A close friend of hers.'

'Well, I'm sure that won't happen with me.'

But was she? He'd already taken advantage of a slip on her part to kiss her. Who could say what would happen next?

After that small disagreement, the evening passed without further discord. As Lauren had expected, she enjoyed the food, a considerable improvement on the lamb chops she'd planned to be eating. She'd been in time to collect her order — just. Tom hadn't been there but Sam had. He'd been a bit friendlier, even asking, 'How are you? Nice to see you again. Your order's ready,' and he'd handed her a neatly wrapped package.

She'd taken it and paid him.

'Thank you, Lauren,' he'd said.

Wow, he was even using her name. Things were looking up. Maybe she'd been right and he had simply been shy. His manner tonight had been open and warm. He'd even bid her a breezy goodbye. 'See you again soon — hopefully.'

'Oh, I'm sure you will, Sam. After all, we live practically opposite each other.'

She'd been just about to leave again when Tom had walked in. Sam had disappeared into the back room, so Lauren and Tom were alone. The older man jerked his head in the direction in which Sam had gone and whispered, 'I think you've got an admirer there. He's just too shy to say anything.' He winked at her.

It wasn't until Lauren was climbing the stairs to her flat that for the very first time, it occurred to her — could her stalker be Sam? He was a bit of an oddball, so could stalking her be his equally odd way of courting her, without getting too close for fear of rejection? If it was him, he surely hadn't realised how troubling such a method would be.

No, it didn't make any sense. Because why would he park a car outside in the street and sit in it, watching her window, when he lived practically opposite to her and could see from there? Unless his intention was to trouble her? Scare her, even?

Oh God, could he be unhinged? Unhinged enough to do something like that? His erratic behaviour towards her could be an indication of that. One minute he smiled and spoke, as he'd done just now; the next time she saw him he was just as likely to totally ignore her, if his past record was anything to go by. It certainly wasn't the behaviour of someone rational and sane.

Or could he be hoping that she would be scared enough to run to him for protection? That wasn't too far into the realms of fantasy — or was it?

* * *

Unlike Nicholas, Greg didn't order any champagne, but they enjoyed a fairly decent bottle of French Merlot. Other than at Fiona's party, it had been a long time since she'd done much more than say a few dozen words to Greg, usually in passing on the street. She'd known he worked for an IT company — the rumour mill had seen to that — but she hadn't realised the extent of how well he was doing with them. He told her now that he'd been made overall manager of a new department that would concentrate on creating websites for professional people and companies.

'Next step, MD,' he laughed.

She realised then what a nice man he had become: ambitious but unassuming; confident but without the arrogance that Nicholas at times displayed. And, as long as she managed to keep him off the subject of her employer, he was fine. He entertained her with amusing anecdotes about his workmates and some of his customers, and the evening passed swiftly and pleasurably.

It wasn't until he was driving her home that Nicholas's name was mentioned again.

'I wasn't exaggerating about Jordan, you know. I've made a few enquiries and he's acquired a bit of a reputation as a ladies' man. He likes to love 'em and leave 'em in pretty quick order, so all I'm saying is — be careful with him. Okay? Take nothing for granted. He's pretty ruthless where business is concerned, so he's most likely the same in his private life.'

'I'll be careful, but I'm sure there's no need. I've had nothing to worry about so far.' Which of course was a downright lie, because his kiss had worried her. Not least because of her own disturbing response to it, a powerful desire for more of the same. And now Greg's warning words had provided even more cause for anxiety.

All of which meant that yet again she tossed and turned instead of sleeping. What was happening to her? She rarely had trouble sleeping. Even Sheba eventually deserted her, jumping off the bed and stalking — tail aloft and switching from side to side — out of the room, emitting a bad-tempered-sounding meow as she went.

Perhaps she should, after all, find herself another job. But where? And with whom? There was Greg's offer, but something about it didn't appeal. The sensible course would be to wait and see what happened with Henderson's. If Nicholas did turn out to be the sexual predator that Greg believed him to be, then she'd have to re-think. But till then — well, what was it they said? Better the devil you know — unless of course he did actually turn into a devil.

With her decision made, sleep finally and blissfully overcame her.

* * *

That Saturday she decided to pay a visit to her friend Stella's hairdressing salon. She needed a trim as well as a sharing of confidences, so this way she'd slay both birds with the same bullet. And another visit so soon after the last would keep her friend happy.

There was nothing Stella enjoyed more than a good old gossip, and more to the point — certainly as far as Lauren was concerned at the moment — she had the knack of being able to help her get things into perspective. Also, Stella didn't mind cutting her hair once the salon had closed for the day, which was at four o'clock on a Saturday. Which meant she could confide her doubts about working for Nicholas without fear of being overheard, as well as getting Stella's practical and down-to-earth take on it all.

But the main thing she wanted to talk about was the text messaging and the night-time stalking. Although there'd been nothing happening on either front for the past couple of nights, and she was beginning to hope that whoever it was, given her total lack of response to it all, had called it a day, she'd decided it was time to confide in someone. And who better than her best friend?

But her hope that it had all come to

an end was extinguished when she walked out onto the street and glanced at her car. Beneath one of the wiper blades was a rose; a single, long-stemmed, red rose.

She stared at it. So he hadn't given up, after all. She dashed over to the car and lifted the blade, yanking the rose free, before bending it and snapping it in two. Only then did she stride into Stella's salon.

'Look.' She shook the broken rose in front of her friend. 'I've just found this on my car.'

Stella stared at her, puzzled. 'You've found a broken rose?'

'No, it wasn't broken when I first found it. I've broken it.'

'You broke it? Why?'

And that was the prompt for Lauren to tell her all that had been happening: the man sitting in the car, night after night; the phone messages and texts; the flowers. In a strange sort of way, talking about it eased her anger, at least partially. Which meant she herself was able to put it into some sort of perspective. After all, he hadn't actually threatened her; so far it had all been done from a distance.

Stella stared at her, appalled. 'Haven't you been able to find out who it is? Get his phone number at least?'

'No, he always blocks it and parks his car — or stands as he did last time — away from any sort of street light. It's a small car, some sort of hatchback, I think.'

'You have to go to the police, Lauren.'

'And say what? I've no evidence to prove my story. And without evidence . . . '

'Please tell me you haven't deleted the texts.'

'I kept the last two, but looked at rationally, there was nothing threatening in them. They were almost love letters. The police, from what I've read about other women suffering the same sort of thing, don't seem interested.

The stalker hasn't actually committed any offence, and until he does their hands are tied.'

'Great! So he has to physically harm you first?'

'And then there's Nicholas Jordan . . . '

Stella's interest shifted up a gear. 'Nicholas Jordan? Good grief,' she gasped, 'it's not him, is it?'

'No — at least I don't think so.' But was she sure about that?

'Well, that's something at any rate. You don't want to have to give up your job as well.' She eyed Lauren, her curiosity plain to see. 'How are you getting on working for him? Is he really as bad as everyone says?'

'I haven't really had enough time to judge. The thing is, Stell — well, I've heard a spot of gossip about him.'

'Who hasn't? What is it? Don't tell me — he likes to ravish his PAs?'

'Spot on — well, almost.'

Stella gaped at her. 'I know I originally said he'd eat you alive, but you are joking, aren't you?' She was frowning now. 'Aren't you?'

Lauren shrugged. 'I'm not actually.'

'But — has he tried anything with you? And who told you?'

'Greg Mallory and no, he hasn't tried anything — well, not really.'

'Not really? What the hell does that mean?'

'He kissed me.'

Stella emitted a cry that was an equal measure of horror and excitement. 'He didn't! Well come on, tell me. I want all the sordid details. One of my customers saw him the other day. He's a real hunk, she said.'

'He is attractive in a dark kind of way.' And that was an understatement if ever she'd uttered one.

'So,' Stella urged, 'tell me. What exactly happened?'

'He took me out to dinner — to the Bistro in Kingsford.'

'Way to go, gal.' She punched the air triumphantly. 'Now tell me if I've got it wrong, but I thought you didn't fancy him, and I have to say I didn't have you down for such a fast worker.'

'I've had to be,' she ironically declared, 'the amount of work he expects me to do in a day.' She ignored the comment about not fancying Nicholas. Not even to Stella would she admit how much she'd been affected by his kiss.

'Worth it, though, eh, if he buys you dinner somewhere like the Bistro? I've heard it's pretty fab. So go on.' Her eyes glittered now with anticipation.

'He drove me home afterwards, and I stumbled getting out of the car. He caught me, and that's when it happened. When he kissed me.'

'Tongues or not?'

'Not! It was over before it really started. I think it was just his way of thanking me for all the work I'd put in that day — nothing more.'

'Does he want any extra staff? Because if that's his way of saying thanks, I'm more than up for it. He could even reduce my salary.'

Lauren chuckled. 'You're always up for it.'

'Now, now, there's no need to be cheeky.'

'How is Roy, by the way?' Lauren pointedly asked. Roy was Stella's fiancé.

'Oh you know, the same as ever.' She lowered her shoulders, trying to make out she was less than enthusiastic.

'You've got a good 'un there. Remember that.'

'Yeah, but a teensy bit boring, maybe?' Stella quirked a mischievous eyebrow.

Lauren knew her friend was joking. A more perfectly matched couple than Roy and Stella she had yet to meet.

'Hey, maybe we could do a foursome some time. I could check Nicholas out, see if he's good enough for you.'

Lauren knew what that meant. Nicholas would be subjected to a virtual inquisition. It had happened before and had put off more than one man. All Stella would say when Lauren complained later was a flippant, 'Well, if he can't put up with a few questions, then he's not all he seems to be in my view.'

'But questions about what he wears beneath his trousers?'

'That says a great deal about a man. Boxer style, traditional underpants?' She grimaced. 'Hmm, bit boring. Modern, body-hugging? He's go-getting and ambitious. Dynamic, even. But that's only my opinion, of course. Anyway,' she went on now, 'I'd say go for it. Nicholas Jordan definitely sounds the body-hugger type.'

'You've changed your tune. I thought you had him down as a ruthless predator.'

'Yeah, well, I've since realised he did me a favour making me redundant. I'd never have branched out on my own otherwise.'

'Oh, by the way, I met Serena. She interrupted our dinner, as a matter of fact.'

'Did she? What was she doing back here?'

'Seeing Olivia, apparently.'

'Oh, well that's good, good for Olivia at any rate. Anyway,' Stella went on, a frown returning to her brow, 'to get back to the other thing — the stalking. I really think you should tell the police, see what they say. At least then you've made an official report. And as for the gossip about Nicholas, watch yourself there too, seriously. Don't get yourself into a position where he can take advantage.'

* * *

Feeling calmer since her talk with her friend, Lauren did go to the police station and duly reported all that was going on. And just as she'd predicted, the young PC told her that there wasn't a great deal they could do as things stood.

'Let us know if it gets worse, if actual threats are made.' And that was that. 'You'll probably find he'll lose interest eventually if you just ignore it all. Don't respond in any way.'

Which was easy to say. What wasn't so easy was to ignore the next thing that happened.

Because he was clearly upping his game.

7

A couple of evenings later Lauren turned on her computer, her intention to check any incoming emails. She had just the one, from someone calling himself Wolfman.

Wolfman? Who would call himself Wolfman? Could it be some sort of spam?

Not at all sure that she was doing the right thing, she clicked her mouse on it and opened it. All she could think was, supposing it carried some sort of virus? A virus that could bypass her security system?

But that wasn't what most disturbed her. It was the words that appeared on her screen.

'I don't know why you're ignoring me, not when we're growing so close. Please, my lamb.'

An image instantly appeared in her

head — a disturbing image. It was of a wolf gobbling up a defenceless lamb. Was that what he wanted? Was that why he was calling himself Wolfman? *Don't be ridiculous*, she told herself. *It's just words*. With that in mind, she read on: 'Forgive me for whatever I'm supposed to have done wrong. Was it our little spat?'

What little spat? She frowned at the screen.

'If it was, I'm truly sorry. I love you, you must know that, and sometimes it makes me do and say the wrong thing. I know we can work through this.'

Whoever he was, he must be truly delusional; insane, in fact, and living in a parallel universe to the one she was inhabiting. The chances were they'd never even met, because nobody she knew would do this to her, she was becoming increasingly convinced of that — and as far as having some sort of spat — ? But how the hell had he got hold of her email address? From one of the cards she frequently handed out?

But she had to do that. All professional people did it.

Suddenly, she was tempted to reply and tell whoever it was to leave her alone, to stop this insane stalking. Tell him she'd been to the police. But she hesitated, fingers hovering above the keyboard. Would that simply make matters worse? If she angered him too deeply — which telling him she'd been to the police might do — would he become dangerous? He knew where she lived, and probably where she worked. Supposing he took it into his head to approach her? Assault her, even?

Abruptly, she closed the email — as if that would somehow make it all disappear. She groaned, feeling the beginnings of a headache.

As if sensing Lauren's unease, Sheba leapt up onto her lap, digging her claws into Lauren's thigh, as she prepared herself a spot to curl up. 'Ouch!' Lauren groaned. Sheba took no notice.

'What shall I do?' she asked the cat.

Ignore everything, that was what the

police constable had told her and what her own common sense was telling her. After all, she once more reasoned, he hadn't actually physically threatened her. No, it was the sense of being continually watched that was getting to her; the fact that he was talking as if they were lovers.

Which, not unnaturally, inspired her next question: what would he do if she persisted in ignoring him?

Maybe she should take the laptop to the police and show them the email. But what could they do? They wouldn't want to waste their time trying to discover who had sent it, although she was sure they would be able to. And, let's face it, the words he'd written were nothing more threatening than a declaration of love. They'd most likely think it was simply an ex-lover, someone she'd upset — that she was hysterical and exaggerating what was nothing more than a lovers' tiff. Which of course was precisely what the words implied.

She stared at the screen saver. What should she do? The truth was, she didn't know.

She pushed Sheba from her lap, to the cat's mewling indignation, and strode to the window that looked down onto the street. She yanked the curtains open. If he was there, watching her flat, she'd go out there and confront him. Demand he stopped his ridiculous games.

But she didn't recognise any of the parked cars as being his; in fact, she was pretty sure they all belonged to the neighbours. In any case, she checked her wristwatch. It was only nine thirty, much too early for him. His time was anywhere between eleven and two o'clock. She tugged the curtains closed again and went back to the settee, lifting Sheba up to bury her face in the animal's fur.

* * *

Somehow she dragged herself to work the next morning. She had eventually slept but it had been a fitful slumber, punctuated by a series of dreams; well, nightmares, really. In the final one before she woke, someone — a shadowy figure, the same one that she'd seen standing silently, watching her window — was pursuing her along a dark, narrow alleyway. The buildings on either side had almost touched overhead. It was reminiscent of a scene from a Dickens novel: claustrophobic, suffocating — and full of a dark menace. He didn't speak; he just strode along, his footsteps echoing behind her. No matter how many times she looked back, she hadn't been able to distinguish his face, as a large hood effectively shadowed it. He held something in his hand. A weapon?

Lauren hadn't been able to move easily; her steps were slow, dragging, as if she were wading through thick treacle. And with every second that passed, he drew closer to her. He was within a couple of feet of her, his arms outstretched towards her, when she jumped awake.

She'd sprung up in bed, her body bathed in sweat, her duvet in a tangled heap on the floor. Sheba was nowhere to be seen; she'd probably long ago deserted her. She'd glanced fearfully around the room, half expecting to see the man. Of course, he wasn't there. It had been just a dream, after all, no matter how real it had seemed.

She glanced at the clock. It was just after 5 o'clock in the morning.

She climbed out of bed, knowing there was no chance of going back to sleep. Instead, she went into the kitchen and put the kettle on. The dream continued to vividly play itself out inside her head. She fed Sheba — much to the cat's delight — then made herself a cup of hot, strong coffee. A shower soon afterwards restored her equilibrium. By the time she dressed, she'd managed to banish the relics of her dreams and was concentrating solely on formulating plans for the day ahead.

She had a great deal to do once again, so hopefully the tasks would help her forget her troubled night.

Finally, she regarded herself in the mirror. Not bad. She'd needed considerably more makeup than usual but she wanted to disguise the signs of strain that to her were overwhelmingly evident. Hopefully no one would guess at the sort of night she'd had and ask questions. She was thinking chiefly of Nicholas. He seemed to have an unerring ability to see straight through any excuse she might come up with, and he certainly wasn't above demanding to know what was wrong with her.

She was loath to confide in anyone other than Stella. Because anyone who didn't know her as well as her friend might be tempted to think that at best, she was imagining it all, or at worst, she was losing her mind. For, even she had to admit, the whole thing sounded incredibly improbable. Why would someone like her — a nobody — have a stalker? And, in any case, she couldn't be one-hundred-percent sure, despite what she kept insisting to herself, that it wasn't someone she knew. So it seemed best to keep it all to herself — for the moment, at least.

* * *

She decided to drive to work, even though the morning was a perfect one for early November. A low mist was hanging in the air, depositing sparkling droplets of moisture on the hedgerows and grasses that lined the road once she left the high street behind. It lent the morning a magical, ethereal look.

The clocks had moved back the previous weekend and the days were getting shorter. If she stayed over at the end of the afternoon, as she often did to get things finished, without her car she'd be walking home in the dark; and in the light of all that was going on, she didn't fancy that one little bit. Who was to say someone — he — wouldn't be following her? She shivered as she recalled her disturbing dreams of that night. She fervently hoped they weren't some sort of premonition.

As she passed Jameson's, she spotted Sam sweeping the pavement. She tooted her horn but he didn't look up. She shrugged. Why did she bother? He clearly had no real interest in getting to know his neighbours — at least, not the female ones.

* * *

To her surprise, Nicholas was already in the office that they shared and at his desk when she arrived. It was early even for him. She usually beat him to it by about five minutes or so, and this morning she was early too, so Lord knew how long he'd been here. In her case it hadn't been necessary for her to get in early; she'd simply felt a compulsion to get out of her flat, away from any possibility of being tempted to read another email from Wolfman.

'Lauren — ' He looked up from

whatever it was he was writing down.
' — are you okay?' He frowned. 'You don't look well.'

'Bad night,' she muttered.

'Very bad by the look of it,' he added with his usual bluntness.

'Gee thanks, that makes me feel a whole lot better.'

'Sorry, that was rude — but, well, you do look ill.' His frown deepened as he regarded her. She hadn't seen him since the day after their meal at the Bistro. She assumed he'd been spending the time with Serena and Olivia. Despite his coolness towards his ex-wife in the restaurant, there must be a residual affection between them, surely? You didn't just wipe away years of marriage, did you? Even if it hadn't been that many.

'I'm not sleeping very well.'

'I hope that's not down to me overworking you?'

'No, I can cope with hard work.'

'You would say, wouldn't you?' He did look genuinely anxious.

'Believe me, I would.' Although she knew she wouldn't. It would make her sound too feeble. She needed to steer the conversation away from herself and her lack of sleep, even though she was experiencing an urgent desire to unburden herself about what was happening. 'Um, how's Olivia?'

'She's fine. She and Fern have gone shopping.' He grinned. It softened his chiselled features and made him look younger.

She felt a stab of shocking desire deep in her stomach, a positive yearning for him to hold her, to comfort her.

'Apparently my three-year-old daughter has acquired a wish for some new clothes; designer clothes, no less.' His smile dimmed at that and his features hardened again. 'Thanks to her mother.' He didn't elaborate on that statement. In fact, he looked as if he regretted having mentioned Serena in the first place.

'Is she still with you?'

'No. She's hot-footed it back to her husband. Forty-eight hours in my company is more than enough, apparently.' He sounded bitter.

Lauren had no idea how to respond to that, so she didn't. But it didn't sound as if he and Serena had had a happy time together, and the feeling of relief which that supposition engendered was not only a surprise but also maddeningly irritating. Because she'd decided Nicholas Jordan wasn't for her, so any feelings of attraction towards him had to be firmly stamped on.

'Do you feel up to accompanying me to see a prospective customer? Their order — if we get it — would be very substantial, amounting to tens of thousands of pounds. They're a large jewellery manufacturer and they want a complete re-fit with custom-made machinery. I need you to take notes of what exactly they're talking about, and, well — ' He shrugged. ' — it might do you good to escape this office for a few hours.'

She stared at him. Was he planning to quote for what sounded like some highly technical machinery? Surely he didn't possess the expertise or knowledge. Or — oh, good heavens — he wasn't expecting her to do it, was he? Jonathon had always handled that side of things.

But more than that, the thing that really puzzled her was, why was he being so considerate to her all of a sudden? Oh good Lord, he wasn't the one behind everything after all, was he? And seeing how upset she was, had he had a belated attack of conscience? As crazy as that sounded, crazier things happened.

'Don't look so horrified,' he said. 'I just want to have a look — get some details, measurements, that sort of thing. I shall leave it to Bob to work out the actual figures and designs.' Bob Crossley had taken over Jonathon's role. 'He would have gone but he's fully occupied at the moment on another complicated order, so I said I'd do it and take you along for a bit of assistance and advice.'

'Um, who's the customer?' She didn't like the sound of that. He was going to ask her for advice? She had no more knowledge of the technicalities of what they did than he did; well, other than the basics which she hadn't been able to help picking up over the years.

'Whitley's. Do you know them?'

'Vaguely. Aren't they located somewhere off the M6? It's quite a journey.'

'About two hours, I've estimated. If we leave in — ' He checked his wristwatch. ' — an hour, we can be back here again by five.'

'We-ell, I do have quite a lot of work to get through . . . '

'It'll wait till tomorrow.'

And that was that. By nine o'clock they were sitting in Nicholas's car on their way to join the motorway.

He didn't speak for the first part of the journey, concentrating on safely negotiating the mass of fast-moving traffic and the intermittent patches of low-lying mist, and only answering with monosyllabic replies whenever she made tentative attempts to start a conversation.

She began to wonder whether the entire journey was going to be spent in silence. In the end she gave up trying and sat looking out of the side window.

She was understandably startled when he asked, 'So, why aren't you sleeping well? I know I've asked you before, but is the job not working out for you?'

'No, the job's challenging but fine. I enjoy it.' And she realised that she did, against all the odds. 'It's not that,' she impulsively added.

He slanted a glance at her. 'What is it then? Boyfriend trouble?'

'No, not at all. There is no boyfriend at the moment.'

He arched an eyebrow at her, making her instantly regret her honesty. 'I thought you said the other evening . . . ' Abruptly, he stopped talking as if he realised that he, too, had said too much.

'Anyway, as I believe I said once before, the men around here must be blind. I'd have thought they'd be queuing up.'

'And as I believe I said, I've never met anyone I wished to spend any sort of extended time with. That's not to say I don't get invited out.'

'Yet clearly your dates don't please you.'

'It's not that. Well, I suppose it is partly, but actually I have been out recently with someone.'

'Oh?' He continued to watch her from the corner of his eye.

She wished he'd turn his attention back to the busy road, but it wasn't only that. The keenness of his stare was making her feel uneasy. And why was he suddenly so interested in who she was seeing?

'Yes, Greg Mallory. We had dinner.'

'Greg Mallory?'

'Yes,' she repeated.

'I'm surprised you'd see him. If you want the truth I didn't much care for him — not him or that brother of his.

They were troublemakers, and I can't imagine that will have changed.'

A sensation of disquiet pierced Lauren then. Greg had also expressed dislike of Nicholas but Greg had been much more direct, to the extent of warning her against him. Now she wondered if their mutual hostility was down to a long-ago quarrel — maybe in their school days? Over a girl? It seemed more than likely.

'We've arrived,' he unexpectedly said.

And they had. Lauren stared out of the window in surprise. That had passed quickly. She checked her watch — oh, not that quickly; it was eleven thirty. Oh God, she hadn't dozed off at some point, had she? Before they started talking? She hoped not. The mere notion of falling asleep in front of Nicholas was a deeply disturbing one. But if she had, she prayed she hadn't dribbled — or even worse, snored. Yet knowing him and his outspokenness, he'd have mentioned it if she'd done either.

Still, she swiftly checked the front of her jacket and breathed a low sigh of relief when she saw no sort of staining.

He turned the vehicle sharply left and swept into a huge car park, bringing the Jaguar to a standstill just yards from what looked to be the main entrance to an impressive red-brick modern building. As he did so large drops of rain began to land on the windscreen, just a couple at first before quickly turning into a deluge. She sighed. Once again, she didn't have an umbrella with her.

'No umbrella?' Nicholas remarked. There he went again, reading her thoughts. How many times had he done that now? And would she ever be able to keep anything from him? 'Don't worry, I've got one in the boot. It's one I use on the golf course so it's large enough for both of us. I'll get it.'

Which he promptly did. He opened it in readiness and then held it over her, shielding her from the torrent of water now descending from the heavens as she climbed from the car. Slipping an arm around her, he held her close — closer than he needed to in Lauren's opinion, considering the size of the umbrella — as they walked together into the building.

The second they were inside, Lauren freed herself from his tight hold.

'No need to be in such a hurry,' he murmured, 'I won't eat you.' The glint in his eye reminded her of Greg's warning about Nicholas's sexual harassment of his PA. She hoped he wasn't about to live up to that dubious reputation. She could hardly walk away from him here, miles away from home.

But it was the words he'd used that really troubled her: 'I won't eat you.' In fact, they conjured up the name of her stalker on his email. Wolfman. And what did wolves do? Why — they gobbled up the defenceless lambs. Which had been what he'd called her.

Fortunately, the meeting was an extremely intense and complicated one, with a great deal of discussion and note-taking, besides an inordinate amount of measuring, driving all else from her head. It was four o'clock before they finally took their leave. She was relieved to see that the torrential rain had finally stopped — it had lasted the better part of the day, lashing against the windows and hammering on the roof. There was no way they would be back in Lower Markham by five. Not that it mattered; there was no one waiting for her at home, after all.

As they drove out of the car park, Nicholas said, 'I think we deserve some tea after all of that.'

'That would be nice,' she mumbled, and, as if to endorse that sentiment, her stomach emitted a loud and traitorous rumble.

Nicholas gave a snort of laughter. 'More than nice by the sound of that. Essential, I would have said. I'd forgotten all about your — uh, healthy appetite, shall we call it?'

What did that mean? Lauren sneaked

a glance at him and met a pair of eyes that were dancing with mirth. Was he alluding to her appetite for food, or something much more basic? Her sexual appetite? But what would he know about that? Or had he recognised her response to his kiss the other night for what it had been — a burning desire for more? Her face flamed with embarrassment. What must he think of her?

'Not that I'm complaining. I like a woman who enjoys her food.'

Again, his expression could be interpreted any way she wanted. Her mouth tightened in exasperation. He seemed to take a delight in being deliberately provocative.

'That place looks inviting.' He'd spotted a small cafe on the main street of the last town before they reached the M6.

And he was right, it did. It was called the Cafe Rouge and a rosy glow shone through the window, lightening the gloom of late afternoon, as well as ensuring that it lived up to its name.

What was more, there was a parking space right in front of it. Nicholas took her elbow and together they hurried into the cosy interior. The ambience was every bit as welcoming as it had looked from outside. Red-and-white checked cloths covered the dozen or so tables, and a candle was burning in the centre of each one. They took their seats at the only remaining empty table and within seconds a waitress was standing over them, taking their orders.

'Two cream teas, please,' Nicholas said, without bothering to consult Lauren, thus confirming her on-going suspicion that he had her down as greedy. She said nothing, however; she was far too hungry to argue. And when the plate of scones, the jam and the heaped bowl of clotted cream arrived, she immediately tucked in, doing her best to ignore Nicholas's grin.

'Cup of tea to go with that?' he asked.

'Mmm,' she groaned through a full

mouth, thus inspiring another broad grin. She watched, unable to conceal her astonishment as Nicholas deftly poured the tea and handed her a full cup.

'You look amazed,' he finally said. 'Did you think I wouldn't know how to pour a cup of tea?'

'Um, no. Of course not.'

'Liar,' he murmured. 'I don't expect to be always waited on, you know. I do know how to do some things for myself. I can even dress myself and tie my shoe laces, and have been able to since the age of two — or so my mother has informed me.'

'S-sorry, I didn't mean — '

'No?' He quirked an eyebrow at her.

'No, I can see you're extremely competent — even over technical matters.' She was referring to his expert handling of what had been complicated discussions today. 'And you're a master with the tape measure, into the bargain.' Now it was her turn to broadly grin. Let him see what it felt like to be the butt of someone else's mickey-taking.

'Watch it,' he softly warned, observing her over the rim of his cup. 'Can I assume you're feeling better now? You certainly look better. I'll put that down to my expert wielding of the teapot.'

'I do feel better, thank you.'

His gaze was suddenly a serious one. 'So what's really the matter? What's stopping you from sleeping? It's obvious something is worrying you.'

'Oh . . . ' She shrugged, once again resisting the temptation to confide in him. 'You know, life in general.'

'Is it Mallory?'

'Greg? Good heavens, no. He's a perfect gentleman.'

'Family problems then?'

'Not really.' She'd have to tell him something; he evidently was going to press her until she did. The trouble was she didn't know what she was going to say. It had to be something plausible. Then, inspiration struck. 'Well, if I'm honest, things have never been great between my parents and I, um — my father and I have never enjoyed the closeness that you and Olivia have. He's a cold man who really shouldn't have had a child, especially not a daughter. He might have been more paternal with a son.' She was aware of his expression then. It was one of compassion and something else — a previously unseen warmth; tenderness, almost. 'And now they've retired to Cornwall so I hardly see them. I suppose that bothers me. I miss my mother. And what with a new job and a new boss — ' She gave a shrug and a sideways smile. ' — it would be nice occasionally to have someone to talk it over with.'

'Don't you have any siblings you can turn to?'

'No, there's just me. Sad, isn't it?' She pulled a wry face. 'What about you?' Hopefully her question would distract him away from the subject of her. She didn't usually like talking about herself, not in such depth, but somehow she'd felt at ease with

Nicholas; confident that, for once, he wouldn't make judgements.

Of course he knew precisely what she was doing, but he didn't remark on it. 'A younger brother and my parents. They all live in Sussex.'

'Do you see much of them?'

'Not as much as I'd like.'

Her look was an enquiring one.

'They didn't approve of Serena and me divorcing. Not that they were close to her — they weren't. It's Olivia they worry about.'

'She must miss her mother.'

'Do you know, I don't think she does. She was very young when Serena left, just eighteen months, so she's only ever been used to it being just the two of us.'

She found herself thinking, so the little girl's charm must be something she'd learnt from Nicholas, not Serena? Maybe she'd got him all wrong.

'Don't misunderstand me, she loves to see her mother, but . . . ' He paused reflectively. 'She never asks for her in between visits.' He looked at his watch.

'Anyway, it's time we were going. Will Mallory be expecting you?' His question was casually asked but something in his expression told Lauren that her answer mattered.

'No, we've only seen each other once.'

Was she imagining the look of satisfaction that fleetingly crossed his face then?

'Okay. Have you had enough to eat?' This was asked in the lightest of tones, but even so, Lauren detected the hint of sardonic humour. And no wonder: she'd consumed the better part of the cream tea.

'We-ell . . . ' She feigned doubt and watched as astonishment took the place of the humour. She couldn't resist a grin too. 'I've had plenty, thanks. Not even I, with my ginormous appetite, could manage another morsel.' It was her turn to be sarcastic.

He burst out laughing. 'Okay, I asked for that, didn't I? I will never, ever refer to your appetite again.'

Somehow, though, Lauren doubted that.

8

The rest of the drive passed quickly; even so, by the time they reached the factory, it was dark: pitch black, in fact — a direct consequence of the heavily overcast and subsequently moonless evening.

'Where's your car?' Nicholas asked her.

'Parked round the back, in the farthest corner.'

'Okay, come on — let's go.'

'Really, there's no need for you to come with me.'

'I think there is. It's very dark round there. I'd rather see you safely to your car.'

She didn't argue any further, conceding that he did have a point. Maybe she should suggest erecting some sort of lighting. John Henderson had always maintained, whenever that was suggested, that there was no need. He hadn't wanted to spend the probably substantial amount of money to have it installed, she'd suspected.

It only took a couple of moments to reach Lauren's car. She was glad of Nicholas's hand supporting her by her elbows, especially when she tripped over the uneven tarmac. She would most likely have fallen but for his grip on her.

'Thank you for coming with me. I know it's been a long day,' Nicholas said once they reached her car.

'It is part of my job,' she told him.

'Well, anyway, thanks.' He lapsed into silence then, but made no move to return to his own vehicle. He also didn't remove his hand from her elbow.

Lauren regarded him, her head tilted backwards, almost mesmerised by the nearness of him. She was still frozen in position when his one hand lifted, cupping the back of her head, as he gently positioned her for the kiss that she sensed was coming.

His slate-grey eyes smouldered from beneath heavy lids as his head swiftly dipped, and then his mouth was on hers: hard, bruising . . . searching. His other arm tightened around her as he pulled her closer. Close enough for her to feel every line of him, the sheer power of him; the unmistakable evidence of his arousal. She felt helpless beneath the surge of desire which filled her — and that was her only excuse, she later decided, for what she did next.

Her hands crept up his chest and her fingers intertwined at the nape of his neck, as her lips parted beneath his. She pressed herself against him, making no secret about what she wanted — for him to go on making love to her. It was all it took to make him deepen the kiss, his tongue sliding sensuously between her lips as he forced her head backwards. His mouth then abandoned hers and began a slow slide down the length of her arched throat to the pulse that beat so fast in the hollow at the base.

She heard someone groan and realised it was her.

'Lauren,' he throatily murmured, 'you're so . . . ' His hand had moved to caress her, tenderly enfolding a breast. Her breath caught in her throat.

What the hell was she doing? This was her employer she was kissing with such abandon — and, what was more, allowing to fondle her in such an intimate way. She pulled away, simultaneously pushing at his chest.

He stopped what he was doing instantly, and frowned down at her. 'What? What's wrong?'

'What's wrong?' she cried. 'What do you think you're doing?'

He looked stunned for a second, then he gave a snort of amused disbelief. 'Don't you know? You must have been kissed before.'

'Of course I've been kissed before,' she snapped, 'just not by my employer.'

'What the hell difference does that make? I'm still a man, and you're a very lovely woman.'

Desperate to get away — she was so embarrassed at the strength of her response, knowing it would have left him in no doubt of the depth of her feelings for him — Lauren widened the gap between them and fumbled for the key which was in her coat pocket. She then struggled to open her car door — in vain. The wretched thing simply wouldn't turn. It was stuck; jammed. She gasped, muttering under her breath, 'Wretched thing.' It was almost a sob.

Nicholas didn't say a word. He simply placed his hand over hers, stilling her frantic movements, and taking hold of the key. 'It was just a kiss, Lauren. Nothing to get het up over.' And he opened the car door with effortless ease.

Stung by his casual remark, she swivelled her head and stared at him. Was that all it had been to him? Just a kiss? Well if that didn't say it all. He was just a heartless philanderer. Greg had been right. Shame, hot and intense, suffused her then. And she'd permitted him to do it; actively encouraged him to do it, in fact, after that first stunned second. And he'd taken full advantage of that.

'It wasn't just a kiss; it was sexual harassment,' she hotly accused, desperate for some sort of justification for her fury. 'Not just a-a kiss.'

'What?' He went perfectly still, his features hardening, his grey eyes turning to steel. 'Well,' he snorted, with what sounded dangerously like contempt, 'if you want to view what we just did as sexual harassment I'm afraid that's your problem, not mine. Good night, Lauren.' He strode away from her, his back rigid with what she took to be absolute fury.

Lauren watched him go, the despair she experienced in that awful second all but felling her.

What had she done?

She'd practically called him a sexual predator. Practically? She *had* called him a sexual predator.

* * *

Somehow she got into her car and drove the short distance to her flat. By the time she got there, though, she was literally quivering with fury. He'd tried to make it all her fault. How dare he? She hadn't been the one to make the first move; he had.

She needed a drink, a real drink. She opened a bottle of wine that she'd been keeping for when she had some company and poured herself a glassful; she drank it straight down. She immediately poured another and drank that too, but a little slower this time.

She then undressed and put on her dressing gown before going to her laptop. As she did most evenings, she checked for incoming emails. There was just one again. It was from Wolfman. She clicked on it and opened it. The words sprang out of the screen at her.

'Why aren't you answering my emails? I love you. You love me. Please — if you don't respond I'll do something bad. Something you'll wish I hadn't. Then how will you feel? I don't like being ignored, or rejected. Remember that.'

Lauren read and reread the words before, with an angry stab at her keyboard, she closed the email. For the first time, it contained a definite threat. It made for a fitting end to a difficult day. A quiver of misgiving passed through her as she wondered what he meant by 'I'll do something bad'. To himself, or to her?

However, threat or no threat, she had no intention of replying. The police constable had been right; that would only encourage more of the same. What was it they called it? Cyber bullying? Cyber stalking? If she ignored him, surely he'd get tired of such a fruitless game.

But despite shutting down the computer, she couldn't rid herself of the lingering suspicion that it was Nicholas behind it all. Especially in the wake of her rejection of his kisses and then her subsequent accusation. And it was more than coincidental that this email should appear immediately afterwards. For let's face it, this was harassment of a different sort, but it was still harassment.

* * *

The next morning she phoned the office, hoping Sandra, one of the receptionists, would pick up. For the first time ever, she was going to phone in sick. Before this, she'd always managed to go in no matter how ill she felt. Today, however, she couldn't face either work or Nicholas, not after what had happened between them. Because she'd become more and more convinced that, in the wake of her allegation, he'd almost certainly sack her. What else could he do? No employer would be able to countenance such a thing.

But it wasn't just that that bothered her. She had her house rental business to provide her with an income. All right, it wouldn't be as good, but she'd have more time to develop it; acquire more houses, maybe. No, what really bothered her was that she no longer felt she could trust him. For the first time, it seemed highly probable that he was her stalker. Although why he'd be doing such a thing she couldn't imagine. He must have women galore chasing him. Because let's face it, he had everything going for him: good looks, loads of money, a fantastic house. But if her suspicions were correct, then she was working for her tormentor, and her accusation of sexual harassment would pale into insignificance alongside that.

But apart from all of that, she felt genuinely ill. Her head was aching, as was every joint. Her throat was sore and a glance in the mirror revealed a complexion the colour of skimmed milk, as well as eyes that were shadowed and heavy. She didn't think she was suffering from a hangover from the night before, she hadn't actually drunk that much. After just two glasses, and they hadn't been large glassfuls, she'd felt sick. So she'd screwed the top back on the bottle and replaced it in the fridge.

It wasn't Sandra who answered the phone but another girl, Julia. Lauren breathed a low sigh of relief. She'd been scared that it would be Nicholas; he did sometimes pick up the phone if he happened to be near it when it rang. She didn't think she could face his possibly sardonic remarks, not this morning.

'Julia, it's Lauren.'

'Lauren. Is something wrong? Only you're usually in by now.'

'I'm going to have to take the day off.'

'Oh, dear.'

'Yeah, the flu — or something masquerading as it. If I spend the day in bed I should be okay again by tomorrow.'

'Do you need anything?' the kindly woman answered. 'I could pop over.'

'No, no, I'm pretty well stocked up with paracetamol, but thanks anyway. Will you tell Mr Jordan?'

'Yes, of course. It's strange but he's not in yet either.'

'Oh? Maybe he's been delayed.' Or maybe he couldn't face her either. 'Anyway, I'll hopefully see you tomorrow.'

* * *

In fact, Lauren did return to bed, closely pursued by a loudly purring Sheba. The cat was obviously anticipating a day spent curled up on the duvet alongside her mistress. Lauren didn't mind. The feel of the animal, warm by the side of her, was a comfort. It was like having a hot water bottle, one that wouldn't grow cold and need refilling.

The one drawback was that her headache was intensifying by the second. It felt as if she had a brick pressing down onto the top of her skull, an extremely heavy one. She'd taken two paracetamol but it hadn't helped, just as it hadn't helped with the aching of her joints.

Eventually she fell into a feverish sleep and, not unexpectedly, she began to dream once more. She was being pursued along the street, and the person chasing her was the same one as before. And just like before, she couldn't see who it was. He was calling her name this time, over and over. It was a man's voice. Wolfman?

She awoke with a start and a heart that was thundering, to realise it was someone at her door.

'Lauren? Are you in there? It's Nicholas.'

She sat bolt upright, making Sheba leap, startled and loudly protesting, onto the floor. Lauren's head instantly began to spin, with the result that she felt extremely sick.

She groaned. Nicholas was the last person she wanted to see. That was one of the reasons — the main reason if she was honest — she hadn't gone into work. A lot of good staying at home had done her. Couldn't he take a hint, for goodness sake, and just leave her alone?

Thoroughly irritated, she wondered what to do.

She half sat, half laid, paralysed by indecision. Sheba took up a position again at her side, sitting upright, head cocked to one side, listening. If she let him in, would she be letting in her stalker? Memories of her dream — well, nightmare actually — resurrected themselves. She groaned softly. 'If only you were a dog. A big, savage dog,' she muttered to her cat. 'I could set you onto him. You'd soon see him off.' Mind you, knowing how deeply Sheba hated men, all men, that could happen anyway. She gave a shaky smile at the image that that conjured up: Nicholas being chased away by a relatively small cat.

Oh, this was ridiculous. She'd have to let him in. Knowing Nicholas, he'd keep ringing and knocking until she did just that. Sighing, she climbed out of bed. Straight away her head began to spin. She immediately sat down again. Sheba meowed at her and rubbed herself against her arm. Instinctively, she'd sensed that Lauren was out of sorts.

'Lauren, are you in there? Open the door — please. I'm concerned about you.'

Somehow she managed to creep out of the bedroom into the hallway and open the door, Sheba hugging her heels. Nicholas stepped inside the moment she did so. She staggered backwards in her haste to get away from him, which was a stupid thing to do given her unsteadiness. Because if it hadn't been for Nicholas reaching out and making a grab for her, she would have fallen for sure. Throughout all of this, Sheba had been energetically spitting and hissing.

Still holding on to her, Nicholas looked down at the cat. 'Not very friendly, is she?'

'She doesn't like men.'

'Oh yes, you said. Of course that doesn't surprise me.' He repeated what he'd said on the occasion he was referring to. 'Like mistress, like pet.' And he raised both eyebrows. 'She's not likely to make any wild accusations, is she?' He glanced down at Sheba once more. 'Or worse, launch an attack on my ankles?'

With that, Sheba gave a twitch of her tail, another low growl, and haughtily headed for the kitchen.

'Oh no,' Lauren groaned weakly, 'I haven't fed her.' She jerked herself away from him. His proximity was doing all sorts of crazy things to her senses.

'Never mind that for now. You look terrible,' he then went on to exclaim.

'So you keep telling me,' she muttered. 'It doesn't make me feel any better.'

'Sorry. Come on, I'll help you back to bed. Have you called your doctor?'

She shook her head — the wrong thing to do. The nausea surged uncontrollably in her throat. 'No, I must feed Sheba — Oh no, I-I'm going to be sick,' she groaned, and made a dash for the bathroom, it being closer than her en-suite.

To her utter horror, she heard the sounds of him following her. 'N-no, please don't . . . '

He completely disregarded her protest. She didn't have time to say any more; she only just made it to the toilet, whereupon, to her complete humiliation, she stuck her head down the bowl and threw up — violently and at some length.

Once she'd finished — Nicholas had again kept hold of her throughout the whole disgusting business — she began to helplessly weep. 'S-sorry,' she managed to say.

'Don't be,' he gently admonished, holding her close to his chest. Lauren could only pray she wasn't stinking of vomit. 'Come on, back to bed. Lean on me.'

Oh, good grief, was all she could think. Of all people to be witness to her utter breakdown, and then to have help her into bed, it had to be him.

Once she was lying beneath the duvet again, Nicholas disappeared and came back with a large glass of water and a damp face flannel. So she was stinking. Her only wish then was to be allowed to quietly die.

He sat on the bed and, to her astonishment, very gently wiped her face and hands before asking, 'Where do you keep the phone number for your doctor's surgery? I'll give him a call, and then I'll feed your cat.'

Sheba had appeared once more — she'd scooted out of the way while Lauren had been so sick — and was meowing loudly.

'There's no need to call the doctor, really. It's a touch of flu.'

'Right, I'll call mine then.' He pulled his mobile phone from his pocket.

Lauren didn't have the strength to go on protesting. She simply told him where to find the tins of cat food and closed her eyes, meekly lying there, waiting for whatever was going to happen next. She was pretty confident that Nicholas's doctor would refuse to come out to her, so she was astonished to hear Nicholas giving someone her address.

He switched off his phone and, standing up again, said, 'He'll be here in ten minutes. I'll wait.'

She could see no point in arguing with him, so she didn't. Then, unable to summon the strength to do anything else, she closed her eyes and fell instantly asleep. The next thing she was aware of were voices — men's voices. She opened one eye to see a stranger standing by the side of her bed.

'Ms Bradley,' the stranger said with a smile, 'I'm Doctor Francis. Now, let's have a look at you.'

She glanced furtively around the room then, but Nicholas was nowhere to be seen, thankfully. She wouldn't have put it past him to stay and supervise proceedings. He was starting to look like a control freak. A pang of guilt stabbed at her. Maybe that wasn't fair. How many men did she know who would have held her while she was projectile-vomiting? Not one.

The doctor examined her and said, 'You've been rather sick, I hear, and you do look poorly.' He thrust a thermometer into her mouth, removing it again after a moment or two to minutely examine its reading. 'Mmm, nothing too dramatic. I think you've got the bug that's been doing the rounds. I'd advise bed rest, plenty of fluids, and you should be up and about again in forty-eight hours.'

And that was that.

Nicholas showed him out before returning to her bedside, Sheba astonishingly and meekly following him. It was a complete contrast to the spitting, hissing virago she'd been just moments ago.

'She seems to have taken a fancy to me,' he pointed out — with a distinctly smug smile, it had to be said. 'Now, are you okay for paracetamol? Because I'll go and get some.'

'I've got plenty, thank you. I'll be all right now. If you want to go . . . '

Lauren was staring at her cat. Nicholas was right, she had taken a fancy to him. She was rubbing herself against his leg. Unbelievable. Did every female he encountered fall at his feet, she wondered irritably — even the feline ones? It would seem so — apart from her, that was. Which was a really stupid thing to think, because she'd remained quite willingly in his arms — for a while, at any rate.

She returned her gaze to her employer and noted the frown lowering his brow. 'I don't like the look of you.'

Again? she thought. He did have an annoying habit of telling her how bad she looked. She remained silent, however, mainly because of a complete lack of either the energy or the will to argue.

'I think I'll stay for a while longer.'

'No, please — there's no need. I'll just sleep,' she protested drowsily. 'I'll be fine by tomorrow.'

Nicholas ignored that. All he asked was, 'Is there anyone I can call for you? Because if there isn't, I'm staying. You shouldn't be alone.'

'No, there's no one.' And she realised that there really wasn't. How sad was that? Well, there was Stella, but she'd be at work. 'I'm so tired,' she murmured. As if to emphasize that, her eyes closed and she sank into a deep sleep. A sleep that miraculously was empty of disturbing dreams. Once or twice she did partially awake and was conscious of movement in the flat, as well as the absence of Sheba at her side, but her exhaustion was such that she almost immediately lapsed into unconsciousness once more.

* * *

When she awoke some time later, she believed she was alone. The flat was silent; there were no sounds of anyone moving around. She couldn't even hear her cat.

Gingerly, she sat up. She actually felt better. Maybe all she'd needed was a prolonged period of undisturbed sleep.

She swung her legs out from beneath the duvet and slowly stood up. The room swayed briefly but then settled. Still feeling slightly shaky, she left the bedroom and walked into the small sitting room.

Nicholas was there, looking perfectly at home in on the settee, writing on a large notepad balanced on his knees, Sheba stretched out at his side.

Unbelievable, she once again decided.

She was about to turn and creep, unnoticed, back to the bedroom when something must have alerted him to her presence, because he glanced up and saw her. He laid the notepad on the arm of the settee and stood up. Sheba, disturbed and dislodged, immediately grumbled.

'Hush, Sheba,' he commanded, before smiling at Lauren and saying, 'You're looking a lot better. You've got more colour.'

'I feel better. I didn't think you were still here.'

It was after two o'clock, after all. Didn't he have business to attend to?

'Oh, I've been keeping myself busy and Sheba company.' He smiled again. It illuminated his entire face. 'Actually I've got a lot done — no interruptions.'

She stared at him. Was that a dig at her? Did she interrupt him? His expression didn't indicate that, because all of a sudden he looked younger, more approachable. Was that down to his warm smile, or the fact that he was here in her home? Surely she should feel threatened in the wake of her suspicions of him? But let's face it, if her fussy, man-hating cat had taken to him, there couldn't be very much wrong with him.

'Um, I'm fine now, so if you want to go . . .'

He cocked his head and studied her intently. Lauren was instantly aware of what she must look like. Her hair was tousled from sleeping so soundly

— mind you, it persisted in going its own way whatever she happened to be doing, so no change there. Her face was bare of makeup, plus she was wearing a rather ancient and over-sized T-shirt which she was sure must be creased and a bit smelly. And just to complete the unappealing picture, her feet were bare.

But Nicholas didn't seem to notice; either that, or for once he was too much of a gentleman to mention it — which was a miracle in itself. He wasn't usually backward in remarking on how she looked.

He grinned at her and said, 'You look about twelve years old.' He reached out and pushed a lock of hair back from her face.

'Um, Nicholas, I-I'm sorry about last evening.'

He arched a quizzical eyebrow at her. 'Oh?'

'Yes, a-about accusing you of-of — you know — sexual harassment.'

His expression darkened. Lauren

flinched, expecting to feel the full force of his displeasure. But all he said was, 'Ye-es, not something I've ever been accused of before, I have to say. Still, I'm very pleased to inform you that your cat clearly doesn't share your view.'

'No, I can see that. I hadn't realised she was such a fickle creature. Anyway, I'm sorry. I didn't really mean it.'

'Did you not?'

'No.'

'Tell me, I'm curious. Do you accuse all the men who try to kiss you?'

'Of course not.' She was all indignation now.

'Just me then?'

Lauren didn't know what to say to that. She could hardly tell him she'd been completely thrown — threatened, in fact — by her powerful feelings of attraction to him that his kiss had revealed.

To her not inconsiderable relief, however, he seemed disinclined to pursue the matter, saying instead, 'Well, if you're sure you're going to be okay . . . '

'Yes, really,' she eagerly said. 'I think I'll have a bath.'

A dangerous-looking gleam appeared in his eye at that, and she nervously wondered what was coming now. She didn't have to wait long to find out. Because almost at once he murmured, 'Maybe I'd better stay then and oversee that — for safety's sake only, of course. Don't want you passing out in the water and no one here to rescue you.' The gleam transformed itself into a twinkle as he noted Lauren's look of complete horror, and he gave a snort of laughter. 'No need to look so appalled. I was only joking.'

'I-I know,' Lauren stammered. But did she? She wouldn't put anything past him now — not after the way he'd followed her into the bathroom and held her while she was sick.

'But nonetheless, I'm sure it would be a sight worth seeing,' he concluded, still in a throaty murmur. His gaze smouldered now as it swept over her.

Again, Lauren had no answer to that. What she did do, however, was cross her arms protectively over her breasts, convinced he could see straight through the T-shirt to what lay beneath. So convinced was she that he could, her body began to tingle with anticipation and her breathing quickened. It was as though he were touching her. God, what chance did she have against him if by just a look he could reduce her to a state of quivering arousal? None at all, she decided.

And he was still staring at her. Could he detect her emotions? She wouldn't be at all surprised. However if he could, he made no comment other than to say, 'I'll get off then. Don't return to work until you feel one hundred percent better. We don't want whatever you've had infecting the other staff.'

Lauren tightened her lips in vexation. And there she'd been, believing he was concerned for her. How stupid, how naïve, could she be? She frowned. Yet if he hadn't been concerned about her, why had he spent the better part of the day here, watching over her?

One thing she did know: Nicholas Jordan was proving to be a total enigma, capable of changing personality and mood at the drop of a hat. To keep people — competitors — off balance? To allow him the upper hand? She wouldn't be surprised.

'I'm sure I'll be fine by tomorrow,' she muttered.

'Okay. Goodbye then, and take care of yourself. Maybe I'll see you tomorrow. Bye, Sheba. It's been nice meeting you.' He bent and stroked the cat's head. Sheba set up a loud purring, nestling her head into the palm of his hand.

'Traitor,' Lauren whispered.

And that was that. He was gone.

Lauren enjoyed a long soak in the bath and felt more or less recovered by the time she climbed out again. She returned to her bedroom with just a towel wrapped round her, one that barely covered her; but as there was no one to see her, it didn't matter. She grinned to herself. She wondered what her handsome employer would have made of it if he'd still been here. Probably taken it as an invitation to kiss her again. Just the notion — ridiculous as it was, because she wouldn't have done such a thing if he'd still been here — was enough to cause a response within her: a thrill that passed right through her, setting her aflame with anticipation and longing once again.

She went to the window that overlooked a couple of small fields; they were backed by a broad stretch of woodland. The sun, she saw, was already sinking to one side of the trees, bathing them in a golden glow. She loved this view and spent ages gazing at it.

Something glinted unexpectedly in the dying rays of the sun. It came from the edge of one of the fields, the one that ran parallel to the lane beyond. What was it?

She squinted in an effort to see more clearly. Why — someone was standing there, his back to the hedgerow, and he was using a pair of binoculars. That was what was glinting, the glass lenses.

She ducked behind the curtain and then peered out again. It was definitely a man — a man with a baseball cap pulled down low over his face; and the binoculars were trained unmistakably on her window.

He was watching her. And here she was, wrapped in just a towel, and a pretty scanty towel at that.

She gasped.

Could it be the same person who'd been watching her from the car, texting and emailing her? If it was, how many times had he done this, unnoticed by her? Because her bedroom wasn't overlooked by any other buildings, she often walked around with just a small towel covering her.

Horror clutched at her as she sank

down into a huddle on the bed, pulling the towel tightly around her. How long had he been there, watching out for her? And if it had been a while, how could it be Nicholas? He had better things to do, not least managing his many business interests — didn't he?

But if it was Nicholas — and the doubts wouldn't be stilled — she'd been here alone with him all day. How did she know he hadn't spent time in her bedroom, watching her as she slept?

9

Come the next morning, she felt an overwhelming need to escape the confines of her flat, as comfortable as she'd made it. Everything felt spoiled for her, her sense of security destroyed by the knowledge that someone was covertly spying on her in what should be the last word in privacy and safety: her bedroom.

Something occurred to her then.

How had he known she'd be at home at that time? She wasn't usually. Did he wait there for as long as it took, watching out for her? How many times had he done it before? And if he had done it before, why hadn't she noticed him? Of course, Nicholas had known she was at home. He'd been there just before.

Get a grip, she told herself. She didn't know for sure that it had been her the man had had his binoculars trained on. It could have been someone innocently bird watching. She scoffed at her foolishness. Of course, it hadn't been that. The binoculars had been trained indisputably on her bedroom window.

She'd walk to work; it might take her mind off things, and she felt a quite desperate need for both exercise and fresh air after her day in bed. The morning promised a nice day with the early mist giving way to a clear sky as the sun started to rise and burn it off. Nonetheless, bearing in mind how ill she'd felt the day before, she decided to take no chances; she put on a thick jacket and a scarf as well as the sturdiest pair of shoes she possessed and set off. She might not look her stylish best, but she didn't want to succumb to a chill in the aftermath of her bout of sickness.

And she did feel a little shaky and cold to begin with, but that quickly vanished and she was soon striding out, feeling stronger with every step she took. She was about halfway to her destination when a car pulled up alongside her. It was Greg.

'Hey there. How're you doing?' he hailed her.

She grinned at him, surprised at how good it felt to see him. 'I'm fine, and you?'

'I'm good. Can I give you a lift?'

'No, thanks, I'm enjoying the walk.'

'Oh, right. Um . . . I was wondering, would you fancy having a drink this evening?'

'I'd like that.'

And she genuinely would. In fact, she'd have accepted an invitation from Lucifer himself rather than be forced to spend the evening alone in her flat, constantly worrying and wondering if she was being watched; afraid to look out of her window, front or back; waiting for the next text message or email.

'Okay. Eight o'clock in the Frog?'

'Great! I'll see you there.'

* * *

Her arrival at work was greeted by Sandra and Julia with anxious concern.

'Are you sure you're fit to be back?' was Sandra's initial question.

This was followed by, 'You look very pale,' from Julia.

'I'm fine, really,' Lauren assured them, before asking what she really wanted to know. 'Um, is Nicholas in yet?'

'No, he rang to say he's got to go to Birmingham to see someone. He doubts he'll be in today at all.'

Lauren was surprised at the depth of her disappointment at being told that, when in fact she would have expected only heartfelt relief. For the truth was, he'd seen her at her very worst the day before; and in light of that, she'd been dreading having to face him — or at least, she thought she had.

'He also said that if you still look unwell we're to send you straight home again.'

'I'm completely recovered,' she told them. But clearly Nicholas was still worried about her passing on any sort of infection to other members of staff. Dismissing him from her mind — well, almost — she went into the office she shared with him and sat down in front of her computer. She had loads to do, having missed a full day yesterday, and keeping herself busy would, she was sure, distract her from other more worrying concerns.

The day passed swiftly and productively. She'd heard nothing from Nicholas and five o'clock arrived without him having put in an appearance. She didn't even get a phone call from him, and that inspired another piercing of disappointment. Surely he could have called, if only to ask her how she was feeling. Maybe he really didn't care, after all.

She left finally, feeling more than a little let down. Nonetheless, her spirit lifted when she thought about her date with Greg. She'd enjoyed her evening with him at the Bistro. However, her walk home proved more tiring than the morning's journey and she regretted not bringing her car — especially as darkness had descended. She strode as briskly as she could, taking into account her weariness, and wasn't too long reaching her flat. Sam, as usual, was standing in the doorway of the shop on the opposite side of the road. Did he watch out for her? More often than not, he was there when she got home. That idea induced a pang of unease as she recalled the image of the man watching her in her bedroom.

Even so, she called, 'Hello, Sam.'

'Hi, Lauren. You're late.'

'Yeah, I walked. Crazy, huh?' But she couldn't help thinking, so he did know the time she arrived home.

He didn't answer her, however. Instead, he turned and went back inside.

Well at least he spoke now, and that was a definite improvement. Despite that though, she felt another pang of uncertainty. Could he have known she was at home all day yesterday? She supposed he might have done. But he would have been at work, so the theory that the man with the binoculars might have been him didn't really stack up. Unless he'd taken time off?

Dismissing the idea as absurd — Sam might seem a little strange but surely he was harmless — she decided to call in and say hello to Stella; the salon lights were still on. She opened the door to find her friend industriously sweeping and tidying up before leaving.

'You're busy,' she remarked.

'You could say that. I don't think I've stopped all day.' Stella's glance sharpened as she studied Lauren. 'You okay? You look tired; washed-out, even.'

'It's been a long day. Still, I'm off out in a while.' She hesitated, undecided whether to tell Stella about binocular man or not. If she did, she'd be bound to start nagging her to go to the police again, and Lauren, given the total lack of interest on the part of the constabulary, couldn't see the point. She decided on that basis to say nothing.

Stella's interest intensified. 'Oh yeah? Where to? A hot date, is it? Oh God — ' Her eyes widened. ' — not a date with the hunky Nicholas?'

'No, I haven't seen him today. I'm meeting Greg Mallory for a drink at the Frog.'

'Are you? I haven't seen him in ages — or his brother, come to that. What was his name?'

'Paul,' Lauren absent-mindedly told her.

'Yeah, I remember now. How are they both?'

'Fine — well, Greg is, I don't know about Paul; the last time I saw him was at Fiona's party. Did you know he'd been working in the States?'

'No, I didn't.'

'He's back now, and looking for a job apparently.'

Stella eyed her friend. 'So Greg's still keen on you, is he? You dated him for a while, didn't you? Are you about to get back together?'

'No, definitely not. We're both long over that.'

'Mmm, maybe you should give it a go. There hasn't been anyone in a while. Of course, he's not in hunky Nicholas's league, I'll give you that — but he's reasonably nice-looking.'

'I s'pose.'

'Don't sound so enthusiastic, will you?'

'I'm joining him for a drink. What more d'you want? Anyway, I only popped in quickly. I'll see you.' She gave her friend a hug.

Stella had always been a bit of a matchmaker, Lauren mused as she left the salon. She simply couldn't help herself. If she was happy, then she wanted her friends to be the same. But truth to tell, Lauren would never view Greg as anything other than a friend. She frowned then. She hoped he didn't have any ideas about reviving a romance between them, because that really was a non-starter. Maybe she shouldn't be encouraging him by going out with him.

Thoroughly weary now and wishing she hadn't agreed to meet him, Lauren slowly climbed the stairs to her front door. She fitted the key into the lock and, when it wouldn't turn, discovered the door was already open. She frowned. Had she forgotten to lock up behind herself this morning? That wasn't like her, especially under present circumstances. If anything, she'd become a bit OCD about it.

She turned the handle and pushed the door wider, more than a little tentatively it had to be said. Once inside she listened for any sort of sound, but when a swift glance around saw no signs of any sort of break-in and the door didn't look as if it had been forced, she could only presume it had been an oversight on her part. Which just showed the sort of mental state she was in.

She took her jacket off and then her shoes before fetching a ready meal from the fridge and putting it into the microwave. Not that she was particularly hungry, but if she was going to be drinking, she'd better have something to eat.

Once she'd finished her meal she had a shower and began to dress for her date with Greg, selecting almost absent-mindedly a pair of tailored trousers and a favourite sweater. She then opened a drawer, intending to pull out one of her many scarves — a pale grey one with tiny rosebuds printed on it — to drape round the V-neck of the rather plain jumper.

Strange; it wasn't there.

She reached to the back of the drawer in case it had been pushed back by something else. She rummaged around but it definitely wasn't there. She clicked her tongue in vexation as she tried to recall where she'd put it that last time she'd worn it — or even when she'd last worn it. She searched the other drawers but still couldn't find it. Could she have left it somewhere? She must have done. That was irritating; it was one of her favourites. Oh well, it would turn up sooner or later. She pulled out one of her others instead.

She went to her dressing table and, bearing in mind Stella's remark about looking washed-out, applied a further thin layer of makeup and then added some more blusher. Satisfied with how she looked, she reached for her favourite perfume.

That wasn't there either.

She frowned. She always kept it alongside the mirror and never moved it, other than to spray it on herself, of course.

A prickle of unease began within her then. A missing scarf; her perfume nowhere to be seen. An unlocked door when she'd been sure she had locked it.

Had someone been in here? Someone who had a key? But no one other than she had a key. Not even Stella.

Her heart began to pound in her chest as she began to go through her belongings to see if anything else was missing. Nothing was, at least as far as she could see. Her jewellery was all still there. Okay, so it wasn't valuable, but she still would have thought a thief would help himself simply because it was there and would probably fetch a few pounds. A silver-backed hairbrush given her by her grandmother just before she died and which was quite valuable was also still in its place. Again, surely a burglar would have taken few of the other things just lying there and not been content with a mere scarf and some perfume?

She rushed into the sitting room, only to discover that everything was there too: her laptop, the television, her CD player.

She stood in the middle of the room and stared around her. The intruder had to have been someone who only wanted a couple of personal things rather than anything of value. Her stalker? It had to be. Yet there was no way he could have got hold of a key. Had he forced the door; picked the lock? She hurried back to the front door and opened it. She then minutely examined the wood around it. Nothing; no marks, no scratches. No sign of forced entry.

Nicholas.

The name sprang into her head. He'd been here for hours yesterday. She'd been sleeping, but he could have taken the things then. He could also have taken her key and had a copy cut. There was a shop a little way down the road that offered that service. She wouldn't have heard him leave and return again, and it would only have taken a few moments. She always left the key in the lock while she was at home — and it had still been there this morning.

The spare key.

She hurried to her bureau and opened it. No, it was still there, so he hadn't taken that.

She all but fell into the nearest armchair. And she'd believed he was staying with her because he cared about her. But why would he have let himself in, using a key, and then forgotten to lock the door again behind him? It didn't make sense. Unless he wanted her to know he'd been in?

Well, she'd put a stop to whatever his or anyone else's game was. First thing tomorrow morning she'd have the lock changed. Then whoever it had been, if he wasn't skilled at picking locks, wouldn't be able to get back in. For the key — if indeed he had had another cut — wouldn't fit.

But she couldn't shift her feeling of unease. Supposing he returned this evening? No, she couldn't imagine whoever it had been would return that quickly — he'd probably got what he wanted for now — but just in case, she'd set a booby trap: a tiny sliver of card placed between the door jamb and the door. It wouldn't be noticeable, unless you looked for it, that was; but if it had fallen out when she got home, which it would if the door had been opened, she'd know someone had been in and she'd call the police. They'd surely have to take her seriously then.

As she walked to the Frog — it lay just a little further along the high street from her flat and the short walk was along a well-lit road — she couldn't stop going over and over the question of who could be doing these things to her, as well as ponder the question that if he was prepared to steal from her, what else might he be prepared to do? Assault her? That possibility despatched a chill right through her — especially if the perpetrator was Nicholas.

Yet, as she'd told herself several times before, Nicholas had his faults, and plenty of them, but she simply couldn't understand why a man of his wealth and substance would be wasting his time stalking and sending anonymous messages — let alone letting himself into her flat and taking her personal things when he could have taken them yesterday while she slept.

So if not Nicholas, who?

She went through the list of other men that she knew. There was Greg,

Tom Jameson, Sam. He definitely maintained a close watch on her comings and goings. Tom Jameson she discounted. He'd never shown the slightest interest in her, and he was what, thirty years older than her, and married with grown-up sons. So that left Greg. She'd given him her phone numbers and her email address, but she simply couldn't imagine him tormenting her in such a manner. Not when he could just invite her out. Of course there were her old school friends, quite a few of whom still lived locally, and whom she saw occasionally. But, as in Nicholas's and Greg's cases, she couldn't visualise any of the men stalking anyone. They mostly had girlfriends, and a few were married.

But then again, it could be someone she didn't know, as she'd considered before. And in a way that would be more acceptable — if having an unknown stalker, or any sort of stalker, could possibly be considered acceptable. But the truth was, she might never know his identity until he actually physically attacked her.

If it was a stranger, then he would have to be skilled in the art of picking a lock to gain entry to her flat, because he wouldn't have had the opportunity of getting hold of her key and having a copy cut. Yet, despite the practical difficulties, it was all beginning to seem horribly plausible. He'd only have had to pick the lock on one door — her front door — because the street door was never locked; didn't lock, in fact. It was purely for access to the flats on either side of hers.

It could be done.

* * *

Greg was waiting for her in the pub. He waved to her as she walked inside. He'd managed to secure a table for two in the far corner of the room. A fire crackled in the grate alongside of him, sending out a welcome warmth and creating the sort of cosiness that Lauren loved. If she could have, she'd have had an open fire in her flat, but it just wasn't possible. For one thing, there wasn't a chimney. Maybe one day she'd have a house with fires in every room. Luxury. She sighed longingly, refusing to contemplate the amount of work that would be involved in that.

'What will you have?' Greg asked.

'A glass of dry white wine, please.'

Greg went to the bar to fetch it for her, thereby giving her the opportunity to check her mobile phone for any messages or texts. Nothing. A tiny ray of hope made itself felt. Could it be that whoever was sending them was, in the absence of any sort of response from her, beginning to grow weary of the game? Yet that seemed unlikely if she was honest with herself, because hadn't he, that very day, gained access to her flat, by whatever means, and helped himself to her possessions?

'Here you are.' Greg sat down and raised his glass. 'Cheers. I've had a head start I'm afraid, so you'll have to work pretty hard to catch up.' He grinned cheekily at her, reminding her of the Greg from their school days. He'd always had the knack of making people laugh and, in fact, she was laughing at a joke that he'd cracked when who should walk in but Nicholas — accompanied, moreover, by a stunningly beautiful woman. Lauren offered up a silent thank-you when the two of them chose seats around the corner from her and Greg, because she really didn't feel like seeing — or talking — to Nicholas. After all, as she'd repeatedly asked herself throughout the day, how would he be able to help picturing her as he'd last seen her: sick, ashen-faced, dressed in well-worn night attire, and throwing up — a complete mess, in other words?

It didn't take him long to spot her, of course, on his way to the bar for drinks. She watched as his gaze left her and moved to Greg, and she then also watched as his eyes narrowed and his expression darkened. It was perfectly clear that he didn't approve of her being with Greg — although what business it was of his she couldn't have said.

He strode across to them and asked, without any polite preliminaries at all, 'Are you sure you're well enough to be here?'

Lauren felt Greg stiffen at her side. She glanced nervously at him, only to see his eyebrows rise quizzically at her. He knew nothing about the previous day's illness. She gave him a weak smile, but when she spoke it was to Nicholas.

'I'm fine. I've been at work all day.'

'Not spreading the infection, I trust?'

'I wouldn't think so.' Could she be sure of that though? She swallowed nervously. He'd blame her, for sure, if anyone else fell ill.

His still-narrowed gaze roamed over her. 'You're still pale. I would suggest — ' At this point he regarded Greg, as if the fact that Lauren was here was entirely his fault. ' — that you get home and go to bed. You need your rest; you were very sick, and looked awful.'

Lauren began to feel irritated. There he went again, telling her how bad she looked. What was his problem? And who did he think he was, telling her to go home and go to bed? He only employed her, for God's sake; he didn't own her. Maybe she should point that fact out to him. As well as the fact that she was a grown woman, not a child to be ordered about.

However, her nerve failed her at that point and instead she said, with deliberate firmness, 'I-I'll be fine, as I've already said.'

'Hmm.' He subjected her to another searching glance before saying, 'Well, if you're positive.'

'I am.' She paused and then added, 'I'm sure your companion must be wondering where you've got to.'

'Probably,' he riposted. 'In which case I'll bid you a good night and see you tomorrow. Bright and early. There's a great deal to do.'

Once he'd gone, Greg asked, 'What

the hell was all that about? Have you been ill? And how does he know how awful you looked?' He was watching her closely.

'I was ill yesterday; too ill to go to work,' she quietly told him.

'And?' His tone was a demanding one.

Indignation coursed through her. What gave these men the right to believe they could interfere in her life, and assume that they should know every detail of what she'd been doing?

And why on earth should she have to tell Greg about Nicholas turning up at her door? It was none of his business. 'I rang work, and — '

'Yes? And?' Greg was sounding impatient now, she supposed because she was being deliberately evasive with her answers.

'Nicholas turned up.' The words erupted of their own volition entirely. Now why had she told him that? She certainly hadn't intended to.

The inevitable happened, of course.

Greg frowned. 'Where?'

'At my flat, of course,' she bit out.

'Why?'

'He was concerned, he said.' She hoped he wouldn't press her to tell him more.

'Yeah, right. Concerned that one of his employees wasn't at work earning her wage — being the slave-driver he's reputed to be.'

Lauren felt driven to defend Nicholas at that juncture. Why, she didn't know. He'd been every bit as annoying as Greg now was. 'I don't think it was that at all. He was very kind; he-he stayed.'

Greg stared at her as if she'd just sprouted horns and a tail. 'He stayed? How long for?'

'Most of the day. I-I was asleep for most of the time, so he got on with some work.'

'Well, I've heard everything now. Nicholas Jordan taking on the role of nurse.' He snorted with derision.

'He didn't nurse me as such. He just made sure I had water to drink. His doctor said . . . ' She stopped talking at the expression that had come over Greg's face. Just as she'd feared she would, she'd said too much — something she occasionally did when she was nervous. Although why she should be nervous with Greg, she didn't know. He had no say in anything. He was just a friend. Maybe she should make that clear.

'His doctor? He actually called his own doctor to you?'

'Yes.' Lauren felt like a naughty child being scolded. For heaven's sake, what on earth was wrong with her? When had she ever let anyone speak to her like this — other than her father, of course? And he'd often spoken to her in the same highly critical manner. It must be due to the after-effects of her illness. 'I was very grateful,' she said. 'I really was ill, and-and I had no one else.'

'There's me,' he burst out. 'Why didn't you call me?'

'Oh, and you'd have left your job and

come running round to me, would you?'

'Well no, maybe not. I couldn't have just walked out.'

'No, exactly,' was all she said to that, 'and I wouldn't expect you to. Do you know, Nicholas is right. I don't feel one hundred percent, Greg. I think I will go home and have an early night.' She hurriedly gulped down what was left of her wine. She'd had more than enough of bossy men for one evening.

Greg promptly followed suit. 'I'll take you — or did you drive here?'

'No, I walked. It's not far.'

'I'll drive you. Especially if you're not feeling well.' He seemed very determined about this and she found herself wondering whether he was trying to compete with Nicholas in the caring stakes. 'I just wish you'd told me you'd been so ill. We could have left the drink for another evening, instead of having to cut it short like this.'

He was right, of course; she had spoilt the evening. In an attempt to mollify him, she said, 'Thank you, Greg. That would be kind of you. I do feel rather tired.'

And she realised that she did, so it wasn't a complete lie. Maybe Nicholas was right and she wasn't fully recovered. But all that reflection did was to revive her fear that she might have passed whatever it was she was suffering from on to her workmates. And if she had, Nicholas was going to be furious.

* * *

Nicholas and his glamorous companion were sitting and talking, heads practically touching, as Lauren and Greg walked by on the their way out of the pub. Nicholas did glance up at them, his expression still one of disapproval, and said, 'I'll see you tomorrow, Lauren. Are you okay to get yourself home?'

'I'm taking her, Jordan,' Greg cut in, 'so you don't need to worry yourself.

I'm sure you have far better things to do with your time.'

Lauren felt her face flame. Did Greg have to be quite so rude? Nicholas was simply demonstrating concern for her.

'Very well, look after her then.'

Greg halted at that and swung to face Nicholas, his expression and intent only too evident — he was set on confrontation. Lauren did the only thing she could think of — she clutched at his arm, murmuring, 'Greg, let's go. I really don't feel well.'

To her relief, he did as she asked and they left the pub and headed for Greg's car parked a little way along the road.

However, Greg couldn't contain his anger and he burst out, 'Damned cheek! Does he think I'm not capable of looking after you? If that isn't absolutely typical of his type.'

She didn't ask him what Nicholas's type was, not wanting to inflame the situation any further, because he did seem overwrought; uncharacteristically so. Instead she said, 'No, I'm sure he doesn't think that. It was a polite remark, that's all.'

'I'll ram his next supposedly polite remark down his throat — so help me.'

Greg seethed all the way to Lauren's. He really did dislike Nicholas. Could it be because she'd had a crush on him all those years ago? Maybe Greg believed she'd ended things with him because of that? Which was completely untrue. She'd been long over Nicholas by then.

He turned the engine off and turned in his seat to face her. 'It's been nice — well, it was until Jordan turned up and stuck his blasted oar in. We'll do it again, hmm?' He smiled then, a smile of such warmth it was as if he'd never displayed such anger. His charm had returned in spades. 'When you're feeling better.'

Lauren smiled nervously. He, like Nicholas, was a man of many facets, and those facets could change with alarming speed. It was unnerving.

'Come here,' he said, putting an arm about her shoulders, pulling her closer to him — well, as close as it was possible to be in the front seat of a car.

'Um, Greg — '

'Quiet,' he whispered. 'I like you, Lauren, really like you — I always have. You broke my heart when you finished with me.'

'I'm sorry, Greg, but I wasn't ready for any sort of relationship — not then.'

He looked at her, his expression one of hope. Why had she said such a stupid thing? And sure enough, he asked, 'Does that mean you are now?' His head moved closer. He was going to kiss her, that was as clear as the stars in the sky above, and she didn't want him to.

But his hold tightened on her and he slid his other arm around her waist, pulling her against him, as his mouth urgently searched for and found hers. 'Lauren,' he moaned against her lips, 'I still want you — even more now than I did eleven years ago. You've grown so beautiful.'

'No, Greg — please.' She tried to

avert her mouth from his, at the same time trying to free herself, but she failed on both counts. He clung on so tightly she couldn't move.

'Come on, just one kiss,' he muttered. She could sense his passion rising. She shuddered, knowing what was coming. His mouth closed on hers, and he forced her lips apart.

She gasped and pushed him away. She felt physically revolted. 'No, Greg — no.'

He stared at her from eyes that were blazing, whether from passion still or anger, she couldn't have said. 'Why not? What's the harm in a kiss or two?'

'Nothing, it's just — ' She paused, and the perfect excuse struck her. ' — I'm probably still infectious.'

'Oh, come on,' he scoffed. 'If you don't want to just say so. If it had been Jordan kissing you, you wouldn't have pushed him away, would you?' His top lip curled when Lauren didn't respond. 'Well, your silence speaks for itself. Clearly not,' he sneered.

'No, that's not — '

'Oh come on, Lauren, I wasn't born yesterday. You fancy him; it was as plain as the nose on your face this evening. You were practically drooling.'

'No, Greg, you're wrong. I simply work for him, that's all.'

But even to her own ears, she sounded unconvincing. Because if it had been Nicholas trying to kiss her, would she have pushed him away? She'd done it once, but the truth was she simply didn't know if she'd have the strength to do it again.

'Look, I really am tired. It's been nice.' She opened the door and climbed out, her relief at doing so overwhelming.

But she wasn't to escape that easily.

'Nice? Nice? Thanks a bunch, Lauren. Talk about faint praise — oh, what's the point? Good night.' He spat the word at her. 'Sleep well,' was his final angry retort before he turned on the engine and toed the accelerator three times, making enough noise to wake the entire neighbourhood. Then, with his wheels spinning, he roared away.

Lauren watched him go with dismay. The last thing she'd wanted to do was upset Greg. But on the other hand, she hadn't wanted to encourage him either. For the truth was that his kiss had left her totally unmoved; there'd been no stirring of passion, no hint of desire: a stark contrast to how she'd responded when Nicholas had kissed her. And that thought brought no comfort at all.

10

Someone was calling her name.

'Lauren? Are you okay?'

Lauren looked up to see Sam leaning out of the window of the flat above the butcher's shop. He'd obviously witnessed what had just happened. Again, she wondered whether he'd been watching for her. He had the perfect vantage point from the other side of the road, after all, to view all her comings and goings. He could well have seen her leaving the flat in the first place.

'I'm fine, thank you.'

'You don't look it. Was that chap bothering you?'

'No, no, really. Everything's fine.' Which, of course, it wasn't, but she wasn't about to tell Sam that.

'I could come down, see you inside.'

'No, Sam,' she hurriedly said, 'but thank you. That's very kind, but really,

I'm okay. Good night.' With that she walked swiftly across the pavement and on up the stairs to her flat.

Very carefully, she opened her door and as she did so, the tiny fragment of paper she'd left there fell onto the floor, which meant no one had been inside. But — and the thought wouldn't be ignored — if the intruder had been either Greg or Nicholas, they wouldn't have been inside tonight, because both of them had been in the Frog all evening.

When Sheba greeted her in her customary fashion, by entwining herself around her legs, she bent to stroke her pet before moving into the kitchen to put the kettle on. A cup of hot chocolate would hopefully work its usual magic and soothe nerves that were jangling.

She already had her hand out to lift the kettle when her mobile phone buzzed. She had a text message. Her stomach gave a sickening lurch. What now? Hadn't she already suffered enough this evening?

She pulled it from her handbag and studied the screen. The number had been blocked, so the chances were it was her stalker. Should she read it or ignore it?

She couldn't help herself. She opened it and read, 'Happy anniversary, my lamb.'

Anniversary? What anniversary? She stared at the words. His last text had seemed to threaten her. Now this one — he must mad; insane.

She read on. 'I can't wait to see you again, kiss you — I love you. You'll get my flowers tomorrow.'

She turned the phone off and threw it onto the worktop, so angry she didn't care whether she damaged it or not.

'Leave me alone, you madman,' she yelled. 'Just leave me alone!'

* * *

Her dreams that night were even more vivid than usual, and decidedly more scary. They began again with the unknown man following her along the same narrow alleyway as he'd done in her previous dream; and as before, he was hooded, sinister, his steps echoing as he kept pace with her. Before, in the manner of dreams, he was there in her bedroom, towering over the bed, a bunch of flowers — dead flowers — hanging from his hand, and still she couldn't see his face. There was just a black hole where it should be.

She woke with a start. She was alone — no Sheba — and uncovered, her duvet once more on the floor. She shivered — not just because she was cold — and glanced at the clock by the side of the bed. It was just after eleven thirty. She'd only been asleep for half an hour or so. Yet it felt like several hours.

She climbed out of bed, and although she knew she was being foolish, her gaze searched the room for any signs of someone having been there. That was how real the dream had been; how convincing. And let's face it, she said to herself, someone had been able to get in, so why wouldn't he do the same thing at night?

She shrugged on her dressing gown and, with hands that shook, tied the belt in a tight knot — as if somehow that would offer protection against any sort of attack. She then walked into the sitting room. Sheba was curled up in the corner of the settee, peacefully asleep. She sat down by the side of her pet and asked herself, what was she going to do?

The first thing was to have her lock changed. That would hopefully remove any chance of someone letting themselves in. Of course, if he could pick locks — ?

She walked to the window and pulled the curtain a couple of inches to one side and peered down into the street below. The car was there, parked almost opposite her flat. Its headlights were off but the street lights were on. She still couldn't make out the number plate, couldn't get a clear view of it, but there was no mistaking the figure of the driver leaning forward and tilting his head as he looked through the windscreen directly up at her. He must have seen her light come on. She stared down at him. Just like the dream, he wore some sort of hood, ensuring that his features were an indistinguishable blur.

All she could think was, he was out there — watching, waiting — hunched behind his steering wheel; completely anonymous, intent on making her life a misery.

Well, he wasn't going to be allowed to.

Without giving herself time to consider the danger she might be placing herself in, she slipped her feet into a pair of slippers and ran to the front door, unlocking it before she leapt down the stairs to the door that led into the street.

At the exact moment that she opened it, she heard the sound of an engine firing up and saw the car shoot forwards, horn blaring and headlights blazing, dazzling her, and making it impossible to see who was in the driving seat or even what make of car it was.

She stood on the pavement, hugging herself tightly, fury engulfing her as she watched it race by. Somehow, he'd sensed — known she was coming. She squinted after the vehicle and managed to make out two letters of the number plate just before it disappeared from view: VU, and the number 1. It wasn't enough. She hadn't even been able to distinguish the colour. It could have been blue or silver. Or even grey.

Her shoulders slumped. What had she hoped to achieve with her mad dash? The driver was hardly going to wait around once he guessed she was on her way down. The last thing he'd want was for her to identify him. It would remove the element of fear, and that, she was beginning to believe, was what all this was about. It wasn't love, admiration, or obsession, even — it was all about control. Whoever it was wanted to control her mind; dictate to her through fear and intimidation.

Slowly, she returned upstairs. She'd given a cursory glance up at Sam's window, wondering whether he'd be there, watching; he wasn't. The rooms were in darkness — which would seem to indicate that he was in bed. It could also mean, however, that he was out, and the significance of that wasn't lost on her.

As unlikely as she'd previously deemed it, the silent watcher could quite possibly be Sam.

* * *

She was late arriving at work the following morning, having waited in for a locksmith. So not surprisingly, Nicholas was already there when she walked in.

'Hi,' he greeted her, his scrutiny a keen one. 'You're late. Had a bad night again?'

Clearly the makeup she'd applied in such generous quantities had failed to disguise her pallor and the deep shadows beneath her eyes. 'Yes.'

'I trust that's not down to Mallory?' was his next caustic comment.

'No,' she bit back, 'it's nothing to do with Greg.' She stared at him, suddenly struck by the fact that he also didn't look great. 'You look tired too, so I could ask you the same question.'

'No, it wasn't Mallory that kept me awake — at least, not directly.' He allowed himself the ghost of a smile.

'That wasn't what I meant,' she snapped. 'I meant — ' She stopped speaking abruptly. It might not be altogether wise to say what she'd intended, which had been, 'I meant the woman you were with. Was she what kept you awake?' He might think she cared. Even, God forbid, that she was jealous.

'So what did you mean, Lauren?' His tone was rough; demanding.

She'd phrase it another way. 'Just that

— well, the woman you were with — you seemed close.' Close? Huh, that was an understatement. They'd looked intimate, not to put too fine a point on it.

'Oh, that's Isabel. And no, we're not close enough for her to keep me awake. She's a friend — the wife of a friend, actually. Her husband, Jeremy, travels a lot and I usually take her out at least once while he's gone.' He gave a small smile, a maddeningly knowing smile. 'Why, did it surprise you to see that I take a woman out now and again?'

'Why should that surprise me?' She gave a snort of feigned amusement. 'I'm sure you take women out on a regular basis.'

'Are you?'

'Well, yes. You're single. Presumably you have a babysitter on permanent tap in the form of Mrs Hodges. In which case, why wouldn't you go out?'

He leant back in his chair and steepled his fingers beneath his chin. 'Well, you'd be wrong. I don't make a habit of taking women out. I'm not interested in dating.' He paused and lowered his eyelids, thereby successfully shuttering his own thoughts as he watched her. 'Not usually, anyway. There are, of course, exceptions to that now and again.'

Lauren began to fidget beneath his gaze. What did he mean? Exceptions to that, now and again? Did he mean her?

She decided not to rise to his veiled insinuation. She suspected he was teasing her in any case, to see what sort of reaction he could provoke. His eyes were glittering from beneath their heavy lids, their expression unfathomable. Who knew what he was up to? She certainly didn't. She did the only thing she could think of: she headed for her own desk. She had loads of work to do. She'd immerse herself in it and ignore Nicholas Jordan — or at least try to.

After that, silence reigned, but she couldn't help wondering about this Isabel. Were they having an affair? He'd admitted her husband was often away, ergo she probably got lonely. It wouldn't be that surprising if she turned to another man. But would Nicholas really do such a thing, and to someone he called a friend? If he was indeed the sexual predator that she'd so impulsively accused him of being, then she supposed he would.

The rest of the day passed quickly and uneventfully, which left her plenty of time to get on with her work uninterrupted. Nicholas left the office just before lunch and didn't return. He also didn't say where he was going, and she couldn't help wondering if he was meeting Isabel again, to take his pleasure while he could.

She was glad in the end to leave work bang on time for a change. Normally, if she was part of the way through a task, she'd stay late to complete it. Not tonight, though. There was nothing that wouldn't wait until the following day, and she felt a quite desperate need for her own home, her own space, her own company.

* * *

She pulled out onto the road from the car park, slowly, because the stretch here was unlit and narrow, and would remain that way until she approached the village and its illuminated high street.

Once she cleared the exit, she increased her speed fractionally. It was a forty-mile-an-hour speed limit here and she religiously kept to it. But as she drove along the winding road — well, lane, really — she became aware of a car behind her. Its headlights were blazing, shining directly into her interior mirror and bouncing back off the glass straight into her eyes. It quickly closed the gap between them until it looked no more than a few inches away from her rear bumper. Yet the driver made no attempt to pass her, even though there was enough width here to do so, which was what she was expecting him or her to do.

She peered into her mirror, trying to

distinguish the face of the driver, but it was no good. Despite the vehicle's proximity to her, the road was simply too dark.

She swallowed nervously. The vehicle must be practically touching her rear. Even as she had the thought, she felt her car jerk forward. Oh my God — he was actually pushing her along.

She stared ahead, deep apprehension beginning to grow within her. They were approaching a particularly sharp bend in the road. The road had narrowed again, it was no more than a car's width. If there should be another vehicle approaching there was no way she'd be able to avoid it, and she couldn't stop; she was still being pushed forward. What on earth was the driver trying to do? In a head-on collision, even at this relatively slow speed, she could kill herself and the oncoming driver. Her heartbeat raced then as she realised the danger she was in.

And then the thing she'd been

dreading happened.

Headlights beamed from beyond the bend. A car was approaching. Another glance in the mirror showed her pursuer still right behind her. She didn't dare stop — a collision was imminent, one way or another, and she couldn't see how to avoid it.

A horn blared loudly at her, warning her to pull over, but there simply wasn't room, and she still couldn't stop. She was being pushed inexorably forward. Somehow she had to get past the oncoming vehicle. She did the only thing she could: she steered her own car into the thick hedgerow. She could hear the brambles and branches scraping and tearing at the bodywork. Under the circumstances that didn't seem important. And then, by some miracle, somehow she squeezed by unscathed, and all she could see was the furious expression of the driver of the other car as he shook his fist at her and mouthed several, probably rude, words.

It was only a matter of yards then

before the road widened and the lights of the village were blazing just ahead of her. Another swift glance in her mirror showed that the car behind her had pulled back, widening the space between them. She gave a heartfelt sigh of relief right before it closed the gap again and, with a prolonged blare of its horn, finally raced past.

Thoroughly shaken, she pulled to a halt at the first opportunity and then watched as a small hatchback disappeared into the distance.

Who had it been? Her stalker?

He'd never tried to harm her physically before, yet the more she considered what had just happened, and the fact that the driver had seemed to deliberately try and intimidate her — to push her into an oncoming car, in fact — it looked more and more as if he had done just that.

Had the fact that she'd ignored his emails and texts angered him sufficiently to make him want to punish her in some way? One of the texts, the last but one, had certainly hinted at something like that.

In which case, she could only assume he was about to keep his word and dangerously up his game.

11

The first thing Lauren did when she got back to her flat was to check both her emails and her phone for any sort of message from the stalker. Something — anything — to indicate that he'd been her pursuer. That he'd decided, finally, to punish her for her refusal to respond to him. She could then take it all to the police and hope they could discover his identity and stop him before he hurt her in some way.

But there was nothing.

There wasn't even the promised bouquet of flowers waiting for her.

Maybe she should go to the police anyway; take her laptop and show them the emails. Tell them about this evening's events; about the unmistakable threat to her safety. Maybe then they'd take notice and do something? But what, she almost at once asked herself, could they realistically do? They'd hardly put a twenty-four-hour guard on her; they didn't have the resources these days for that. And would they take her word about what had happened this evening, in any case?

It was at that point that she admitted that she was on her own in this. And she posed the question — would he really try to harm her? The unpalatable truth was that, after what had happened earlier, she didn't know, and that was the most alarming notion of all.

* * *

She ran herself a bath, hoping that the hot water would relax her and ease her growing disquiet. She lay back and opened the paperback book that she'd brought into the bathroom with her, preparing to immerse herself in the story and forget, for a short while at least, all that was happening. Sadly, she'd only managed to read the opening couple of paragraphs when she heard her doorbell ringing.

She sat bolt upright, only just managing to keep hold of her book and stop it from falling into the water. She wasn't expecting anyone.

She inhaled sharply as a single thought sprang into her mind. Had her stalker decided to show his hand, and reveal himself at long last? Had he, in fact, come to finish off what he'd started on her way home?

Slowly and with a quickening heartbeat, she climbed from the bath and slipped her arms into the towelling robe that hung on the back of the door. Wrapping it tightly about her, she fastened the belt into a tight knot and left the bathroom.

Another ring sounded — a more prolonged one this time, as if whoever it was at the door had kept his finger on the bell. He was growing impatient.

With her sense of disquiet heightening by the second, she slowly walked into the hall.

'Who is it?' she called. She had no

intention of opening the door until she knew exactly who was out there.

She glanced at the clock on the wall. It was six fifteen. Could it be Stella? She did sometimes call in before going home.

'It's me, Nicholas.'

'And Olivia,' a child's voice piped up.

What could they want?

She took a deep breath and looked down over herself. Her rather shabby bathrobe was hardly the right attire to receive guests in, especially not Nicholas Jordan. He'd be bound to make some sort of derogatory remark. After all, he seemed to have no compunction about pointing out any sort of defect in her appearance. And she really wasn't in the mood for criticism — not this evening. Should she pretend to be out? But she couldn't do that; she'd already asked who it was.

'Just a minute,' she called back. She cast a quick glance over her reflection in the hall mirror and the sight that met her eyes confirmed her worst fears: a bathrobe that was sorely in need of a wash, not a scrap of makeup — she'd removed it before climbing into the bath — cheeks that were flushed, hair tangled and dangling in wet strands from when she'd lain back in the water. A mess, in other words. She could already hear him saying, 'Oh dear, bad hair day?'

With a sigh, she opened the door to find not just Nicholas and Olivia, but Fern too. Good Lord, this was getting worse and worse. She waited for him to speak.

'I was beginning to think you were out,' were his initial words.

If that wasn't just typical. No polite greeting, no 'how are you?' — just what sounded like a complaint that she hadn't immediately run and opened the door. Well, she shouldn't be surprised. He was running well and truly to form. 'I was in the bath,' she muttered. 'You've caught me at a bad time.'

'We've come to see Sheba,' Olivia excitedly put in. 'Can we?'

Nicholas, she noticed, was taking his time in looking her over, his gaze a shuttered one; so shuttered, in fact, she couldn't detect any expression at all; no hint of what he was thinking of her disreputable appearance. Instinctively, she hugged the bathrobe tighter about herself. A suit of armour would have been her preferred choice of attire.

'Ye-es, I can see I've disturbed you,' he finally drawled. 'Sorry — we should have phoned first.'

He didn't sound the least bit sorry, however. Lauren compressed her lips in annoyance. 'That would have been preferable. You'll have to excuse me.'

'What for?' he asked.

She mutely indicated her bathrobe.

'Oh, that — rather fetching, I thought.' He grinned.

It was at that juncture that Sheba walked warily into the hallway. 'Oh, look, Daddy!' Olivia screamed. 'Isn't she gorgeous?' She launched herself towards the cat. Sheba didn't instantly run away, as Lauren expected. Instead she backed off quite slowly, before turning to bolt back into the sitting room.

'Olivia, darling, you're frightening her,' Nicholas gently cautioned.

Lauren interrupted so say, 'Go into the sitting room. She'll probably be more receptive in there.' She wasn't at all sure of that, though, and found herself crossing her fingers behind her back. 'Um, I'll just go and put something on.' Once more, she indicated her shabby bathrobe. She was feeling at a distinct disadvantage compared to the other three smartly dressed people.

'There's no need,' Nicholas murmured, 'and, after all, it's nothing I haven't seen before.'

He was referring to her bout of sickness and seeing her in her night time T-shirt. But whatever it was, it was an extremely intimate remark. She stared at him; his eyes gleamed, but he didn't say anything more on that subject, to her utmost relief. She dreaded to think what Fern would make of it if she should overhear such a conversation.

'Are you all right, Lauren?' he went on. 'You look — '

'What?' Here it came. She looked tired, pale.

'Shaken, I suppose, would be the most appropriate word.'

'I'm fine.' She was dismayed to hear the tremor in her voice.

He cocked his head and studied her closely. 'No, you're not. What's wrong?'

If only she could tell him. But she still wasn't sure he wasn't somehow involved in what was happening to her. For all she knew it could have been him in the car earlier. He'd have had plenty of time to get home afterwards, collect Olivia and Fern, and drive here. But if it had been, then he must have a second, smaller vehicle.

'Nothing,' she said. 'I'm probably in shock at opening my door and seeing you all there.' She made a valiant attempt to laugh it off — not very successfully, she suspected, judging by his expression now.

Olivia had by this time run off after Sheba; Fern had gone with her. Lauren anxiously listened for the sounds of her cat's usual spitting and hissing when anyone she didn't know tried to pet her. But apart from Olivia's crooning words, 'Hello, Sheba. Aren't you sweet?', there was nothing.

'Still, I'd better get in there,' she said, indicating the sitting room doorway. 'I'm not sure how Sheba will react to . . . ' Her words petered out.

'A small girl stroking her? I'll think you'll find, if my experience is anything to go by, that Sheba will be fine. She struck me as a very confident cat, well able to cope with strangers.' He smiled. 'You just have to know how to treat her.'

Stung by his assumption that he knew how to smooth ruffled feline fur and she didn't, Lauren stiffly led the way into the room and saw that he'd been right. When wasn't he? For there was Olivia perched on the settee, Sheba at her side, loudly purring as she allowed herself to be somewhat energetically stroked.

'Daddy . . . ' Olivia regarded her father beseechingly. 'Can I have a cat? She's so lovely.' She pressed her cheek against Sheba's back.

'Oh, we'll have to think about that,' Nicholas said.

'Oh, ple-ease; ple-ease. I get so lonely.' The little girl opened her eyes wide at her father, fluttering her lashes flirtatiously at him.

Lauren had to smother a chuckle; now that she undoubtedly had learnt from her mother. Whoever it was she'd acquired the trick from, it worked. Nicholas gave a resigned laugh. 'I see. Well, maybe we could consider a rescue cat.'

Olivia instantly leapt to her feet, clapping her hands as she jumped up and down. 'Can we go now?'

'No, not right now. They'll probably be closed for the night. Maybe at the weekend, hmmm?'

Olivia sat down again, content for the moment to pet Sheba.

'Fern,' Nicholas then quietly said, 'why don't you take Olivia home? I want a word with Lauren. Here.' He dangled a set of car keys. 'Take the Jag. I'll get a taxi back.'

'Oh, Daddy,' Olivia wailed.

'Yes, Olivia, it's your bedtime. I'm sure Lauren will let you visit again — or maybe she could come to the house and see you.'

Eventually the little girl accepted it was time to go and off she went, manifestly excited at the prospect of owning her own cat.

Once she and Fern had left, Nicholas asked, 'I wondered if you'd like to come and have a drink with me. We didn't have time to talk today. I had to go out rather unexpectedly.'

When he didn't elaborate on that statement, she bit out, 'Yes, it was rather sudden.' He obviously had no intention of telling her where he'd had to rush off to so urgently, and once again she wondered if it was to meet the lovely Isabel.

He looked taken aback by the sharpness of her response. 'Uh — '

'Someone to see? Business to do?' she waspishly asked. 'You clearly didn't need my assistance this time.'

'No.' His one eyebrow arched quizzically at her, as if he was wondering why she was so thoroughly annoyed. 'It was personal business.'

Ah-ha, she thought. She was spot-on. She didn't stop to think about what she was doing. She put her suspicion into words. 'Isabel — again?'

Something gleamed deep within his eyes, something that looked remarkably like satisfaction. She gnawed at her lower lip, waiting for whatever was coming now. Something she wouldn't care for, she guessed. Had she given herself away?

She very quickly discovered that that was exactly what she'd done. 'We-ell,' he breathed, 'not jealous, are we?'

'Jealous? Me?' she indignantly demanded. 'Why on earth should I be jealous?'

'Why indeed? You tell me.'

That maddening gleam was still there in his eye, she noticed. She'd have to tread very carefully. She'd already revealed more, much more, than she intended. She tightened her lips. God, she was stupid. She should have known he'd see straight through any protest she might make.

Clumsily, she tried to cover her tracks. 'Th-there's really nothing to tell. It-it's none of my affair what you do in or out of business hours.'

He cocked his head and regarded her, his gaze moving from her eyes to her mouth. It lingered there until Lauren felt as if he were actually touching her. Her lips parted as her breathing accelerated — all a dead giveaway. Of course he noticed, and another gleam, an infinitely more dangerous gleam, briefly flashed into his eyes.

'You're right, it was Isabel I had to see. Jeremy's left her and she wanted my advice on what to do — as one of his closest friends. She's devastated.'

'Oh.' Now she felt foolish.

'I don't think I was much help; I really didn't know what to say to her. So I was hoping you could help. You know, if I could get another woman's take on it — on how I should handle things.'

'Why would I know what you should say? I don't know either of them, and I've never been in that situation. Look, do you want a drink here, rather than go out?' If she sounded ungracious, she couldn't help it; didn't care, in fact. The cheek of it, asking for her help with regards to how he should handle another woman; an especially lovely woman at that.

'I'd like that. It's been a particularly stressful afternoon, as you can probably imagine. I'm not accustomed to having a woman crying on my shoulder.'

'Oh, aren't you?' She couldn't disguise her scepticism at that statement. She was quite sure he'd had a good few women crying — if not on his shoulder, then certainly crying over him. He was far too good-looking not to have had that experience.

'No. Contrary to your evident opinion of me, I'm not a womaniser. I respect them too much to treat them in such a callous fashion.'

She had no answer to that, so she escaped into the kitchen where she pulled out a bottle of Pinot Grigio from the fridge. In truth, she herself was sorely in need of a drink. Whether as a result of her frightening experience on the way home or the unexpected appearance of Nicholas at her door, she couldn't have said. The latter, she suspected.

'White wine okay?' she called.

'Fine.'

She poured two generous glassfuls, taking a couple of substantial gulps from hers before returning to the sitting room — which was a rather unwise thing to do, having had nothing to eat since her lunchtime sandwich. Of course it went straight to her head, making her progress back to join Nicholas somewhat unsteady.

She handed him his glass and invited him to sit down, indicating the only armchair; she intended occupying the settee opposite. Nicholas did as she suggested.

'Where's Sheba gone?' he asked, glancing round the room.

'Into my bedroom, I expect; on my bed, catching up on some sleep.'

'Oh.' He set his glass down on the low table that sat between them and asked, 'So how do you suggest going about things?'

'Things?' she asked as she took another mouthful of her wine. She was already feeling miles better. Suddenly, nothing looked so bad. The wonders of alcohol, she decided. Maybe she should drink more of it? Things might seem not so bad then.

'Isabel,' he said. 'What should I say to her? What should she do? She wants Jeremy back.'

'Oh — yeah. Isabel. Well, does she know why he's left her?'

'She thinks for another woman, but she has no evidence to support that theory. And I have to say, I have strong doubts about that. Jeremy's never been one for deception and lies. He's never been any good at it for a start. He's a genuinely honest guy; one of the most honest I know. And I would put money on him still loving Isabel.'

'Have you spoken to him? That would seem the first obvious step.'

'No, not yet. I'm afraid of making matters worse if I'm honest.' He frowned. 'He's not going to like me telling him Isabel thinks he's got someone else, for starters. Especially if I'm right and he hasn't.'

'Do they have any children?'

'No, Isabel doesn't want any. Jeremy does though, quite desperately.' He regarded her thoughtfully. 'I wonder if you've just inadvertently hit on his reason for leaving.'

'Ask him; and if it is, then try and get them together to talk things through. Maybe if he hasn't told her exactly how much he wants a family — ?' She shrugged. 'If you could do that, then there's a chance they could resolve the situation; reach some sort of compromise somehow.' It was her turn to scrutinise him. 'Is that what you and Isabel were talking about in the Frog the other evening?'

'For a while, yes. She was upset.'

'Well, I'm sure you consoled her,' she bit out, only to bitterly regret the words a second later.

He gave her a long, level look before asking, 'Why would you say that?'

She took another long swig of her wine. It imbued her with even more bravado, enough to blurt, 'You s-seemed very close — intimate one might almost say.'

Again, he didn't respond straight away. When he did, his voice was low, inflexible. 'Lauren, let's be clear about this. I'm not in the business of consoling other men's wives, and certainly not my best friend's. There are other people I would much rather spend my time and energies on. Two in actual fact, but one in particular.'

He didn't remove his gaze from her, not even when he got to his feet and moved across to the settee. Still not looking away, he sat down by the side of her, sliding one arm across the back of the settee behind her shoulders.

'R-really?' she stammered. 'And who would that be?' Her heart was hammering fit to burst from her chest. Especially when he reached out and took her glass from her to put it down onto the table.

His eyes were mere slits as he asked, 'You mean you don't know?'

She shook her head. Words were beyond her at that point.

'Well, let me tell you. One of course is Olivia; that goes without saying. The other — ' He paused before going on in a low, seductive voice. ' — is you.' He dragged her towards him, to bend his head and claim her already parted lips.

12

Lauren literally stopped breathing. And then, just as had happened whenever he'd kissed her, she began to respond, powerless against the tsunami of desire that rampaged through her. Her lips willingly parted to allow his tongue inside, as his arms tightened around her and he pushed her slowly backwards until she was lying on the settee beneath him. Savagely now, passionately, he ground his lips over hers.

Taking her acquiescence as a sure indicator that she, too, wanted this, his mouth began to trace a pathway down her tautly arched throat. His hand began to slide over her curves, fondling, cupping. Her bathrobe parted beneath his fingers. She gasped, her pulses and her breathing galloping out of control. His hand searched for and enclosed the soft fullness he found there as he groaned, 'Lauren . . . '

She lifted herself towards him, offering everything — everything he so clearly wanted.

Then — what the hell was she doing, again? This was Nicholas Jordan, the man who could quite possibly be her stalker. She struggled to get up, trying to push him off her. 'Stop — stop it — '

He did, instantly. He straightened, allowing her to sit up; his eyes smouldered at her and his brow was pulled down in a frown. 'I thought — '

'What?' she cried. 'What did you think? That because I'm your personal assistant, you can be this — well, this personal?'

'What the hell are you talking about? I didn't expect anything, other than for you to do your job.' He stood up, his eyes blazing.

Lauren swiftly followed suit. She didn't care for the sensation of him towering over her, his features distorted with rage. And, after all, she didn't know what he would be capable of while he was in this mood. Supposing, as she'd just wondered, that he was her stalker, after all? How would he react to this rejection of his lovemaking? If it was him, he'd already placed her in danger.

'Well,' she bit out, 'you do have a bit of a reputation with regard to your PAs.' Her words faltered beneath the granite stare. 'Or so I've heard. And I have to say . . . ' Defiantly she battled on, determined not to be intimidated into an apologetic silence.

But he interrupted. 'Yes? What do you have to say?' The harsh words were ground out from between tightly compressed lips. 'Do enlighten me.'

'Well, it all seems much more believable now,' she lamely told him.

'This is the second time you've accused me of sexual exploitation. Who've you been listening to? No, don't tell me — let me guess. Greg Mallory.' Contempt positively dripped from him.

She didn't respond to that, mainly

because she didn't want to get Greg into trouble, and she wouldn't trust Nicholas not to seek him out and confront him.

'Well.' His expression was a withering one as his gaze raked her from head to foot. Hastily, she pulled her bathrobe closed again — she'd only just realised it was still hanging open, exposing an embarrassingly generous portion of her body to his gaze. 'If that's what Greg — ' He sarcastically emphasized the name. ' — said, it must be true.'

Her face was flaming by this time — with humiliation at the fact that she'd been standing barely covered and he hadn't pointed it out to her. Undiluted anger literally exploded from her then. 'Well, do you deny it?'

'Why should I? What would be the point? You've already tried and condemned me by the sound of it. Not once, but twice.' There was a dangerous glint to his eye now. 'Do you know, Lauren, I'm not surprised you're still single. Not if you fling these wild accusations at any man who dares to kiss you.'

'I — I don't.'

'Oh, it's just me then that you've singled out — twice — for that particular form of character assassination, is it?'

Lauren felt a flutter of uncertainty then. Why didn't he deny it? It would be the natural thing to do. But — maybe he felt he shouldn't have to? Maybe he didn't wish to give substance to the accusation by denying it?

Oh God, could Greg be wrong? Had he, in fact, really heard it? Or had he invented it to make sure she didn't become involved emotionally with her employer?

Nicholas swung, obviously preparing to leave. 'So, as you clearly don't want a serial sexual deviant in your apartment, I'll take my leave.'

'I-I'm sorry, I-I may have been — '

He turned back to face her, his features looking as if they were carved out of stone. 'You may have been what?'

The harshly uttered words felt as if they were practically stripping the flesh from her.

She shrugged. 'Stupid?'

He cocked his head and gave a grim smile. 'Quite. You've listened to someone who only had mischief in mind.' He paused, then went on. 'I just want to make one thing absolutely clear to you.'

She waited, wondering nervously what was coming now.

'I have never, ever pressed my attentions on a woman if she made it clear she didn't welcome them. And I didn't get that impression from you. And most certainly not in those first few moments. You were very — how shall I put it — receptive; eager even, for my kisses. So what happened, Lauren? Second thoughts?' He quirked an eyebrow at her as he awaited her response.

Well, she thought, at least he'd denied it. 'S-something like that. It didn't — doesn't — seem appropriate. Not when I work for you. I've always

taken care not to mix business and — '
She didn't how to describe what had just happened between them.

'Sex?' he sardonically prompted.

'No.' Her denial was instant and adamant. 'Pleasure.'

A glint of something — satisfaction? triumph? amusement? — appeared in the depths of his gaze. 'Oh, so you found it pleasurable then?'

Lauren blushed again and nodded.

'Well, that's something to be grateful for, I suppose.' His tone was once more heavy with sarcasm. 'Okay, I'll see you tomorrow — that's if you're willing to work with a man who has just tried to make love to you.'

Her lips parted in astonishment. She'd been sure this time she'd get the sack.

'And I promise I won't try to kiss you.' He muttered something under his breath, which meant she couldn't make out what he said. It had sounded like, 'At least, not while you work for me.'

If it had been that, what did he

mean? That he'd never, ever kiss her again because she intended holding on to her job?

It was then that an emotion that felt perilously akin to aching disappointment engulfed her. For goodness sake, what was the matter with her? She'd been the one to call a halt to their lovemaking, as he'd described it. Was that what it had been? she miserably asked herself. Because if it was, then did that mean he genuinely did love her?

* * *

Once he'd left, a sensation of unutterable loneliness — abandonment, even — overwhelmed her. She covered her face with her hands. Oh my God. The truth struck her with a force powerful enough to knock her down. She slumped into an armchair. She'd fallen in love with him — deeply and helplessly — whatever the truth of his feelings for her.

She took her hands away from her face, her emotions in total disarray; yet for all that, hopeful. Because he must feel something for her. Otherwise, why kiss her, caress her with tender desire, with such depth of feeling? Because there had been unmistakable passion in him — and not just on his part, she miserably conceded.

* * *

She headed towards the kitchen, where she found Sheba asleep, not on her bed where she'd supposed, but stretched on one of the worktops. Lauren didn't disturb her, although she didn't much care for her being up there. She proceeded to prepare her usual remedy in the wake of whatever was troubling her: a large mug of hot chocolate. After which, she returned to the sitting room, intending to watch some television. Something, however, made her go straight to the window and look down onto the street below.

There was no sign of Nicholas, so he must have managed to get a taxi pretty quickly. She glanced up the road in the direction he would have taken to go home, and there it was — her stalker's car. It was parked a bit further away this time, but there was no mistaking it. She stared down at it. He'd never been there this early — or had he been and she hadn't noticed?

Even as she stood, staring down at the car, thinking it couldn't possibly be Nicholas — he wouldn't have had time to get home, swap cars and return, would he? — her mobile phone buzzed. She'd left it on the coffee table. She went to it and picked it up. She had a text.

She opened it and read the words, her breath freezing in her throat.

'What the hell was Jordan doing there with you? Are you betraying me with him? Did you think I wouldn't know? That I wouldn't be watching? I'm always watching you — you bitch. You traitorous little bitch. I won't forgive you for this. Never, never. You're going to pay.'

She let her breath out in a long, slow hiss. As she'd wondered more than once, had he always been out there — somewhere? Still, it confirmed what she'd just that second decided; her stalker wasn't Nicholas. The relief she experienced then was like nothing she'd ever felt before, reinforcing the fact that she truly loved him. But as the reality of all that had happened blazed at her, she admitted that she'd ruined everything, any chance of him returning her love, by stupidly repeating what Greg had told her; by taking his word over Nicholas's.

She re-read the text message. Whoever it was had recognised Nicholas, which meant it must be someone who knew them both. She looked back down, just as the vehicle's headlights flashed twice and it sped away — not, however, before she'd managed to read the number plate in full. VU13 GTF. And this time she recognised the model. A Ford Fiesta; a silvery blue Fiesta.

She wrinkled her brow. She didn't know anyone who owned a Fiesta, did she? Could she be wrong and he was a stranger? Yet he'd recognised Nicholas, which must mean he lived in the village, or at least nearby.

Well, there was only one way to find out. Even though it was dark, she'd drive through the village, try and spot the car, and hopefully discover who it belonged to. Discover the truth, at long last.

She quickly dressed and went out to her car. It didn't take her long to locate the vehicle. Parked immediately in front of No 1, Rose Cottages, Greg's cottage, was the car, a silvery blue Fiesta, number plate VU13 GTF. She stared at it. That couldn't belong to Greg. Where was his BMW? Unless he owned two cars? One purely for his stalking activities? As she'd also wondered about Nicholas at one point. No, it had to be one of the other cottage owners. Greg wouldn't stalk her; he simply wouldn't. She wanted to believe that so much.

And then Greg walked out of the cottage and headed directly for the blue car.

Determined now not to return home without discovering exactly what it all meant, why he would do such a terrible thing to her, she climbed from her own car and hurried across the road towards him.

'Greg,' Lauren called, 'can I have a word?'

As he turned and saw her, a strange expression crossed his face. Dismay? Fear? Anticipation, even? She couldn't quite pinpoint which it was. 'Lauren? What can I do for you?'

'Can we go inside? I don't want to sort this out on the street.'

'Sort what out?'

Despite his apparent air of unconcern, she could sense how ill at ease he was. My God, it had been Greg.

'Please — can we go in?'

He turned back towards the cottage.

Lauren followed him through the front door and into a small hallway. It wasn't until he was closing the door behind them, and leading the way into the sitting room, that she belatedly questioned the wisdom of being there alone with him. He could well pose a threat — a serious threat once she accused him. He'd already tried once to harm her. And that last text message had indicated deep anger as well as dangerous jealousy of Nicholas.

But this was Greg, she told herself. Surely he wouldn't hurt her. After all, if it had been him, he must love her — in a strange kind of way. Yes, she couldn't stop herself thinking, in a twisted, perverted sort of way.

He swung to face her. 'So what is it?' His eyes had hardened. He didn't look like the Greg she'd always known. He was changing in front of her. She was no longer quite so sure that he wouldn't hurt her.

Lauren shivered. 'Do you know, it's nothing. I'll go. It was a mistake to have come.' She turned to leave. She'd go straight to the police. Let them sort this out. She must have been crazy to try and do this herself.

But it wasn't to be.

Greg reached out and grabbed her by the arm before swivelling her round to face him. 'Oh no you don't, not now I've got you here. I've been dreaming of this.' He glanced around. 'Tell me — what do you think of the cottage? Pretty impressive, huh?'

'It's gorgeous.' And it was. The room they were in had a low, beamed ceiling and an inglenook fireplace in which a fire was burning. The aroma of wood smoke drifted towards her, a deep pile carpet covered the floor, and comfortable-looking furniture invited one to sit down. It was cosy and welcoming.

Or would be, if only she didn't feel so threatened.

She smiled at him, trying to ease the palpable tension that was rising, before glancing pointedly down at the hand on her arm, indicating that he should release her.

And it was then that she saw it: a small scar on his one index finger, his left index finger. Her stomach lurched.

It wasn't Greg; it was Paul, his twin. It had been Paul who'd been stalking her. But why? Greg, she could in a weird sort of way understand, but Paul? They'd had no contact since their school days, and they hadn't had much then. They hadn't even spoken at Fiona's party. 'Is that your car out there?' she asked.

'Yeah. I want something bigger eventually, but . . . ' He shrugged.

She didn't need to hear any more. His words confirmed it. It had all been Paul. 'Look, I've got to go.'

'You're not going anywhere, not now I've got you here — at last.'

And then the words literally burst from her. 'I thought you were Greg.'

'Did you? Oh well, it always was an easy mistake to make. It gave us endless fun as boys.' There was a remorseless, steely look to him now; his gaze was razor-sharp as it rested on her. 'So how do you like Greg's cottage?'

'I told you, it's gorgeous.'

'How would you like to live here — just you and me? I'm sure Greg would sell it to us if I asked him to.'

'Well, I don't know.'

His mouth twisted into a sneer. 'No — it's still Jordan, isn't it? You even ditched poor Greg for him as I recall.'

'No, I didn't,' she quietly said. 'And anyway, that was years ago. We were eighteen.'

He didn't seem to have heard her, so incensed was he. 'And now you're ditching me — before we've even really got started!' he shouted. 'I've tried so hard to show you how much I love you. My messages, the flowers, and still it's not enough.' A dark stain appeared upon his face as his temper blazed. He looked menacing. Crazed.

'Paul — ' Somehow she had to calm him. 'You've scared me half to death. You could have killed me earlier, chasing me in your car. What were you thinking of?'

He looked confused at that. 'No, no — I wouldn't hurt you. I love you. You love me. The way you looked at me at the party. I could tell you wanted me.'

'You spied on me in my bedroom,' she cried. 'You even broke into my flat. How did you get in?'

He smirked. 'Picked the lock; it was dead easy. I learnt how years ago and yours was a very simple mechanism. You women,' he scoffed, 'you're all the same. Sophie in New York, she wouldn't listen to me either. I tried everything, everything!' he shouted, his eyes gleaming with the light of insanity, 'and she reported me to the police. I had to leave, leave my job — my whole way of life.'

He was deeply disturbed, that was becoming increasingly evident. Had he always been that way and no one had noticed? 'How did you get my phone numbers, my email address?'

'How do you think I got them?'

Again he sneered. 'Greg had them in his address book. It only took a quick look.'

'I see. Well, I really do have to go. I'm expecting visitors, and if I'm not at home they'll start looking for me.'

'Are you sleeping with Jordan?' he suddenly burst out. 'He was there with you this evening. I saw him leave.'

'It was just business, that's all. I work for him.'

He ignored that. 'I always wanted you, but you never noticed me, did you?'

'I did.'

'No, you didn't. Don't lie to me.'

Lauren stayed silent. Whatever she said was only fuelling his anger; his madness.

'Well,' he snorted, 'you've certainly noticed me lately, haven't you?'

Where was Greg? If only he'd come home. 'Paul, I must go.' She turned towards the door.

'No.' He grabbed hold of her arm again, his grip a bruising one.

'Paul, you're hurting me. Please — let me go.'

'No!' He grabbed her other arm now and began to shake her. 'I want you to stay. You're going to stay.'

Panic suffused her. She couldn't see any way out. Why had she even come in? She'd recklessly put herself in danger. How could she have been so stupid? 'Just let me go and we'll forget all about this.'

'You want to forget me?'

'No, no — of c-course not. Not forget you.' She gave a shaky smile. 'How could I do that? I want us to be friends.'

'Friends? Friends?' He shook her even harder. Her head rocked back and forth. She began to feel dizzy. 'We're more than friends, don't you know that?' He pulled her into him roughly and began to kiss her. 'This is what I want. I thought you knew that. I told you in my emails.'

Lauren literally froze. Everything she did or said was just making things worse. She stood absolutely still, knowing she mustn't give him any sort of encouragement, although whether that would work she didn't know. It certainly hadn't so far.

But her action — or, rather, lack of it — did finally have the desired effect. He pushed her away from him. 'You cold bitch.'

Lauren didn't hesitate; it might be her only chance. She turned and made a run for the front door, yanked it open, and raced through before he could stop her.

'Lauren, please, don't go — '

The anger, the madness, had vanished. He was a young boy again, being denied that which he wanted. Fleetingly, she wondered if he could be schizophrenic.

'Sorry, but I have to.' Without as much as a glance back at him, she ran out onto the road, praying that he wouldn't come after her.

He didn't, although he did call, 'Don't tell anyone about this, Lauren, or there'll be consequences. Serious consequences!' All trace of the young boy had vanished; he was threatening again.

'I won't, I promise. Bye.'

She had almost reached her car when a man's voice called her name.

Her heart sank. It was Paul. He'd followed her.

13

Lauren looked around.

It wasn't Paul; it was Nicholas. She all but collapsed in relief. He must have seen her running and had stopped his car.

'Lauren,' he called, 'what's wrong? You're as white as a sheet.' He got out of his Jaguar and strode across to her.

'What are you doing here?' was all she could think to ask him.

'I was concerned about the way we parted — and I decided to come back and try and resolve things. When you weren't in, I decided to carry on and see a friend, and then try you again on the way back. You see, I don't much care for being labelled some sort of pervert.' His expression darkened dramatically. 'I noticed your car.' He pointed to where she'd parked it on the opposite side of the road to the cottage.

'Isn't this where Mallory lives?' Anger and suspicion blazed at her.

'How do you know that?'

'I saw him coming out one day.' He was watching her intently. 'Are you and he together now? Is that why you keep rebuffing me, and why you believe his lies?'

She shook her head, speech was beyond her. Delayed reaction to all that she had been through — not just tonight but all the other nights when she'd felt as if someone were watching her — was setting in. She began to shake.

Nicholas reached for her and gripped her arms. She flinched. He'd grabbed her in the same place that Paul had and she was sore. 'Tell me the truth and I'll leave you alone.'

'Paul — Paul's been — '

'Paul?' Nicholas repeated. 'What the hell's Paul got to do with anything?'

Should she tell him the truth? If she did, what would he do? But she simply couldn't stop herself; it all came tumbling out. 'Paul's been stalking me. I didn't know who it was — I've just found out it was him; it was all him . . . ' She began to shake even more violently. 'I-I've been so afraid. He tried to keep me in there. H-he's mad.'

Nicholas stared at her, visibly appalled at what she'd just said. He pulled her in close. 'Tell me exactly what's been going on. Everything.'

'H-he's been phoning, texting me anonymously, emailing me under the name of Wolfman, sitting in his car outside the flat late at night and watching me. He chased me on my way home and almost made me crash the car.'

He held her away from him then, the better to see her face. 'Have you reported this to the police?'

She nodded. 'Nothing they could do, they said.' She began to weep; she couldn't help herself. It was a low-key weeping that she almost at once swallowed back. 'He didn't make any threats until tonight. He saw you leaving the flat and accused me of — of betraying him.'

'Jordan, let go of her!'

Lauren looked over her shoulder as fear exploded within her at what she saw.

Paul was there, running across the road towards them, and he was holding something in his hand.

A hammer.

An icy chill trickled through her. He was going to hurt them. 'It's Paul,' she murmured.

'She's mine!' he shouted. 'Let go of her — you're not having her. No one is.'

'Get into the car,' Nicholas spoke quietly. 'My car, and lock the doors.'

She didn't argue. She didn't have the strength, even though she knew she should stay and face Paul alongside Nicholas. She did manage to stammer, 'B-but — h-he might hurt you.'

'Go,' he murmured, giving her a firm push towards the car. 'I'll deal with this.'

She seemed to have lost the will to argue and she did as he said. She then watched in frozen horror as Paul launched himself at Nicholas, hammer held aloft, ready to strike him. A hammer could kill if used on the skull, couldn't it? Nicholas, however, deftly sidestepped him and, grasping the hand that bore the hammer, shook it hard till Paul dropped the weapon. He then forced Paul's arm up behind his back, and frogmarched him back inside the cottage.

Lauren sat, still paralysed with fear, but also with shock at the sheer strength and expertise of Nicholas's counter-attack. Paul hadn't realistically stood a chance. It was as if Nicholas had been fighting off opponents all of his life. Nonetheless, she waited fearfully for his return. When he finally strode out of the door again, he looked unharmed, even if a little out of breath. He climbed back into the car and sat half-turned, looking at her.

'He confessed to everything,' he told

her, 'and he's promised to leave you alone.' His jaw tightened as his expression turned steely. 'Otherwise he'll have me to deal with as well as the police. He needs help — professional help. He's assured me he'll get it.'

Lauren literally sagged into her seat at all of this. 'Do you believe him — that he'll leave me alone?' She stared, wide-eyed, at the man she had grown to love so deeply and prayed that he would grow to love her back someday when all of this was behind them. Her lips parted in anticipation of that happening.

'I do,' Nicholas murmured. 'Don't look at me like that, Lauren, or . . . ' Slate-grey eyes gleamed at her.

'Or what?' she softly asked. A tiny flicker of hope was starting up inside of her. Hope that she hadn't totally messed everything up between them with her crazy accusations. That there was a chance for them. How could she ever have believed Greg's lies? He would have known that what he was saying wasn't true.

'Or this,' he groaned. He pulled her into him and kissed her lightly on the mouth, before pulling away almost immediately, leaving her unbearably bereft; desolate. Where was the heated passion he'd shown earlier?

He continued to watch her, still holding her, his eyes narrowed. 'I love you, Lauren, and have done practically from the first moment I saw you. I can't hide it any longer — I'm going out of my mind.'

'What?' she gasped. Could she be dreaming? Had she really just heard what she thought she had?

'I was rather hoping you felt the same way.' His expression now was one of uncertainty. 'Although if you have me down as some sort of sexual — '

'I don't, I don't. I never did, not really,' she whispered. 'I'm so sorry, Nicholas. I listened to someone — Greg — when I should have known better. He was jealous of you and he tried to come between us, I can see that now.

Please forgive me. I love you too — so very much,' she murmured, achingly shy suddenly beneath the intensity of his gaze.

He didn't speak for a long moment. Then he tilted his head back and studied her from beneath lowered eyelids. 'Does this mean I'll have to sack you?'

'What?' She was thoroughly confused now. 'Why?'

'Because you told me you never mix business with — now what was it you called it?' His eyes twinkled at her. 'Ah yes, pleasure. And if we're to take our pleasure to the full, you'll have to go.' He grinned at her dazed expression. 'Of course, as Mrs Jordan, you won't really need to work — unless you want to.'

'Mrs Jordan?' she breathed. Was she dreaming? She must be. This couldn't be happening. 'Really?'

'Oh, my darling, yes — really. Lauren, will you marry me? I haven't got the room to get down on my knees, but if we get out of the car . . . '

'Oh, yes, I will — I will marry you,' she cried. 'And I don't need you to get to your knees — not right now, at any rate,' she wickedly added.

'Watch it,' he warned with mock severity.

Something occurred to her then; a possible obstacle to their happiness. She frowned. 'How will Olivia feel about us getting married?'

'How will Olivia feel? She's been nagging me for weeks now to invite you home again. You see, she's fallen in love with you too — although I think Sheba might just have the edge.' His expression softened as his eyes flamed with love. 'Now can we please stop talking, and will you kiss me — properly this time? I think I've waited quite long enough.'

He leaned across to her once more and pulled her even closer to him, whereupon Lauren did exactly as she'd been told.

Other titles in the
Linford Romance Library:

BORROWING ALEX

Cindy Procter-King

Nikki wants to get married more than anything. But what's she to do when her fiancé Royce is dragging his heels over setting a date? Why, fake a fling with the best man, of course! Ambushing Alex may be a tad desperate, but pretending she's hot for him just might kick-start Royce's attention . . . Alex is definitely not on board with this plan. But he quickly realizes Nikki isn't a wild party girl at all. She's cute, sweet — and faithful. Against his common sense, he's falling for her . . .

SEVEN LITTLE WORDS

Margaret Sutherland

Though romance writer Cathy Carruthers has been avoiding men in the wake of a painful break-up, when she meets literary novelist David Hillier neither can resist their powerful mutual desire. But her former partner is hunting her down, and her grandmother's illness means Cathy is landed with her tiny and courageous dog, Pixel. Meanwhile, David has his own problems: writer's block and the care of his father's retired guide dog. Pressures build on the couple, leading to conflict and friction — can they weather the storm together?